CW00920679

COALDUST

Short stories set in a South Yorkshire mining community in the 1930s and '40s

Reg Brown

authorHOUSE®

AuthorHouse™ UK Ltd.
500 Avebury Boulevard
Central Milton Keynes, MK9 2BE
www.authorhouse.co.uk
Phone: 08001974150

First published by AuthorHouse 6/29/2011

ISBN: 978-1-4567-7940-5 (sc)
ISBN: 978-1-4567-7941-2 (dj)
ISBN: 978-1-4567-7942-9 (e)

Table of Contents

Preface

This collection of short stories looks back at life in the mining villages of South Yorkshire during the 1930s and the Second World War. The stories fall readily into two distinct groups as a consequence of the impact of world events. The 1930s was a decade of stagnation, when human progress appeared to be at a standstill and the world seemed to be holding its breath, waiting for something to happen. It was a period which Robert Graves and Alan Hodge wrote of as '*The Long Weekend*'. In contrast, the 1940s witnessed some of the greatest discontinuities in history; the lives of the greater part of the world's population were changed for ever and the British mining communities, although disrupted to a much lesser extent than many, were no exception. Although these stories are fictional, they were inspired by the author's memories of people with whom he came into contact, incidents of which he became aware and influences which he absorbed as a boy growing up in the area.

Coal mining on a large scale came relatively late to South Yorkshire. Although there had been small drift mines and open-cast mining of outcropping coal in the foothills of the Pennines, it was the discovery that the famous Barnsley seam, almost eleven feet thick in places, extended eastward to the Lincolnshire coast and beyond, which brought the enormous expansion in mining that took place in the first two decades of the twentieth century. Some of the new mines were sunk either by or with the participation of coal companies already established in the older mining areas of Northumberland, Durham, Lancashire, Nottinghamshire, Staffordshire and South Wales. Because of the frequency with which new pits were being sunk, there was a severe shortage of miners in South Yorkshire and some of these incoming companies were known to put pressure on employees, in their places of origin, to move to the new coalfield. But stories of the high earnings of hewers in the Barnsley seam soon spread throughout the coalfields of Britain and miners from the older areas came by their thousands of their own accord. To accept them, a company village sprang up around each pit, thereby creating an instant colony of immigrants from unfamiliar places such as Ashington, Wigan, Mansfield, Cannock and Aberdare.

The location of a pit was determined principally by the mineral rights held by the proprietors, but such was the extent and uniformity of the seams that there was usually a wide choice in the location of the pit-head. Considerations such as rail and road communications, commercial infrastructure and social amenities all had an influence, with the result that the pit villages tended to be grouped around an existing town at intervals of a few miles. Some towns were transformed, in the course of two decades, from agricultural communities to large industrial centres, supplying all the needs of their surrounding collieries and, in turn, providing markets for some of their coal. Some mining villages were completely new, whilst others were built as extensions to indigenous communities, the natives of which were not always sympathetic to their new and often boisterous neighbours. By the 1930s, the bigger villages had taken on the character of small towns, becoming Urban Districts under the Local Government Act of 1894, with their own elected councils. Many of the councillors were miners who often formed a Labour majority.

In popular memory, the 1930s are recalled as a decade of unemployment and poverty throughout Britain, but the picture was more complex than that. London and the South-East remained relatively prosperous, as did Birmingham, Coventry and other parts of the manufacturing Midlands. The South Yorkshire of those days could not have been described as prosperous, but its big, efficient coal mines produced some of the cheapest coal in Europe, in consequence of which, many of the pits remained open for most of the time.

The war brought the nation's dependence on coal into sharp focus and increased its demand enormously. Coal was needed for the fighting ships of the Royal Navy and for the merchant fleet which brought in vital supplies of food and raw materials; it was essential for the railways which formed the backbone of the inland transport system and it powered the factories which manufactured the armaments for the fighting forces. After some initial conscription of miners, the Government began to realise that maximum coal output was indispensable to the war effort and, in an Essential Works Order under the wartime emergency legislation, designated mining as a reserved occupation.

Because of the heavy dependence on coal, the mining villages became very important strategic centres, but they were spared some of the worst consequences of the war in that they were too scattered to provide significant targets for the Luftwaffe, few of their menfolk were conscripted and their children did not need to be evacuated.

Reserved occupation status carried with it the duty not to strike and not to be absent from work without good cause. Those who flouted this Order risked imprisonment. It also required reservists to join one of the part-time emergency services such as the Air Raid Wardens, the Auxiliary Fire Service, the Auxiliary Police or the Home Guard. These duties demanded a significant amount of unpaid time, sandwiched between shifts at the pit, at the expense of leisure and sleep. Those young men not employed in coal mining were, of course, called up, so the village had its absent fathers and sons. In December 1941, unmarried women too became liable for conscription. They could express a preference for one of the three women's services: the ATS, the WAAF or the WRNS, or alternatively, the Land Army, the Nursing Auxiliary or approved war work, but their placement depended upon the exigencies of the times. The village was not entirely free of air raids; enemy bombers, bound for the steelworks of Sheffield, passed overhead and occasionally, due either to inaccurate aiming or the jettisoning of bombs on their return flight, the village was hit.

The town changed in character under wartime conditions much more than did the pit villages. It expanded rapidly, not only to service the all-important mines, but to meet the needs of the airfields and army camps in the area and a rash of hurriedly-built armaments factories. The town was also a focal point for the thousands of servicemen and women who were stationed around it. Pubs and dance halls were full of uniforms of all descriptions, not only those of British service personnel, but those of men and women from the Dominions, who had come to support their British cousins and those of refugees from mainland Europe, who had come to continue their fight against Nazi Germany from Britain. In addition, between the spring of 1942 and June 1944, over a million American servicemen arrived in Britain. They came to establish huge airfields and army camps; to support the RAF in bombing Germany and to prepare for the assault on Nazi-occupied Europe. The Americans were polite, generous, gregarious and womanising. They gave rise to that famous lament of British men that the Americans were 'over-paid, over-sexed and over here'. They touched almost every community in the land and South Yorkshire was no exception.

At the start of the war, the attention of the government was focussed on the building-up of the armed forces and eighty thousand young coal miners were either recruited or conscripted before it was realised that such a policy was draining the pits of essential workers. It had not been forseen that, during the course of a prolonged war, the manpower needs of the mines might become more pressing than those of the armed services. That situation arose in the autumn of 1943 and early 1944 saw hundreds of thousands of young conscripts, chosen by ballot, directed without choice into the mines instead of the forces; they were the 'Bevin Boys', named after Minister of Labour and National Service, Ernest Bevin, who, under the emergency legislation, had the power to decide their fate.

World War Two was much more a war of the people than the 'Great War' of 1914-18 had been. Prime Minister, Winston Churchill, described it as 'the war of the unknown warriors'. The whole of the British nation was engaged: not only the armed forces, but every man, woman and child in the land. Air raid shelters had to be built and made habitable, obstacles to seaborne invasion and airborne landings had to be erected, night-time blackout had to be meticulously observed, every person had to become familiar with the use of his or her gas mask, whilst family rations and shortages of almost every conceivable commodity had to be coped with; 'make do and mend' became a way of life. Millions of people were uprooted, not only by service in the armed forces, but by war work, evacuation, enemy bombing and all the other exigencies of war. Emergency services had to be manned: fire watching, air raid precautions and rescue, auxiliary fire service, auxiliary police, local defence, temporary feeding and housing and temporary hospitals. Above all, high spirits and the will to win had to be sustained; the surest way that Britain could have been beaten would have been by a breakdown of civilian morale. The village took these demands in its stride. The war effort was not endangered for want of coal. Some areas saw minor strikes, which could have seen the miners involved going to jail, but the disputes were precipitated by injustices left over from previous decades and were soon settled with a little fairness and understanding. The community, close before the war, drew even closer. The daily urgencies and anxieties inspired a common striving among neighbours; it was their war.

'The village' of these stories is a composite one representing many like it, built over a comparatively short period of time, peopled largely by migrants from other coalfields and displaying wide cultural diversity. The 'town' is typical of the former market towns around which most of the mines were sunk. The characters and incidents were derived from the author's memories of real people and actual events; the stories, therefore, reflect the sort of lives that miner's families led, the diversions they sought, the trials that beset them and the humour that sustained them. Most of the conversations arising in these narratives would have been held in the distinctive South Yorkshire pit vernacular; whilst such dialogue can be enjoyable to listen to, it is tedious both to read and to write and has, therefore, been avoided.

Accounts of colliery disasters and bitter industrial conflict between coal owners and miners are legendary; far less has been recorded about the ups and downs of every day life in a coalfield community. These stories are an attempt to illuminate some aspects of that life by sketching scenes from a culture that has now disappeared from Britain.

THE NINETEEN-THIRTIES

Two Different Worlds

It was Saturday evening. Tony Brooks called for his pal, Tim Marshall, and they set off for their customary Saturday night out, which invariably started with a couple of pints at the workmen's club and finished at the regular weekend dance in the miner's welfare hall. The lads were both in their early twenties, fit and presentable. They both worked underground as fillers, each loading tubs with coal cut by a hewer. Under the 'butty' system, the hewer was paid by the colliery according to the weight of coal he produced and he, in turn, paid his filler a fixed proportion of his wages. Both lads were fortunate in working with high earners or 'big hitters', which meant that their own pay was good. After paying their mothers for their keep, they both had plenty of money with which to enjoy themselves. The biggest difference between the two was that Tony was a talker with always plenty to say in his blunt, Yorkshire way, whereas Tim was quieter and more thoughtful.

With spirits raised by two pints of best bitter, the friends paid their shilling each at the door of the 'welfare', flicked a comb through their hair in the mirror of the gent's toilet and pushed their way into the noisy, crowded, smoke-filled ballroom. They edged slowly around the perimeter of the room, nodding to their friends and keeping a sharp look-out for 'talent'. To them, the girls fell into one of three categories: those in whom, for one reason or another, they had no interest; those with whom they had danced in the past and might do so again, depending on how things turned out and, more importantly, any interesting newcomers. There appeared to be only two new faces: two unfamiliar young women, dancing together, caught the friends' attention by their striking good looks, lovely figures and smart clothes. This was too good to miss. The lads decided to 'split them up' and after a brief debate about who was getting which, sauntered towards them on the crowded floor and asked if they could 'cut in'. Without much show of enthusiasm, the girls agreed and the two pairs stepped off in time to the music. Tony's partner was called Claire. He was pleased to find that she was pleasant, polite and talkative. She and her friend, Laura, lived in a suburb of the town and they had come out to the village dance for the first time to 'see what it was like'. Her father was a solicitor and Laura was the daughter of an engineering company manager. Tim, in the meantime, was making heavy weather in his attempts to have a conversation with Laura. She made little effort to keep the dialogue going and her replies to Tim's questions were either monosyllabic or supercilious. Tim quickly realised that he was not going to get anywhere with Laura.

When the music stopped, the four met up on the edge of the dance floor. Tim was anxious to make his escape, but Tony suggested that they went up to the café on the balcony for a cup of coffee. While Tony was getting the refreshments, Tim did his best to be sociable and offered the girls cigarettes, but neither of them smoked. Almost all of the conversation over coffee was between Tony and Claire. Laura made little attempt to join in and, after a while, Tim gave up trying to draw her out. By contrast, Claire seemed genuinely interested; she wanted to know about life in the village, what it was like down the mine and what the lads did in their spare time. Tony enjoyed himself answering all her questions.

The girls had to leave before the dance ended in order to catch the last bus back to town. The boys accompanied them to the bus stop and as the bus approached, Tim said a quick 'goodnight' and started to edge away, but Tony took Claire aside and asked her to meet him in town one evening of the following week. She agreed and he gave her a quick kiss as she stepped onto the bus.

Tony and Claire met, as arranged, and again the week after that. Tony offered to take her to the pictures, but Claire preferred a chat in a quiet hotel lounge. It was not really Tony's scene, but he would have gone anywhere to please her. Her questions never stopped: she wanted to know about his family, his schooling, his interests and, above all, his job. She had no conception of life underground and wanted to understand it. Her liberal upbringing and education had given her an enquiring mind and the confidence to ask what she wanted to know; her questions became more and more penetrating. Tony answered them with good grace, but he began to feel a bit uneasy about the personal nature of some of them, particularly after such a short acquaintance. When she asked him what he took to the pit for his meal break, his reply of 'bread and dripping or bread and jam' made him wonder how it compared with what she had for lunch in the smart cafés of the town's business area where she worked. When she enquired what he wore in the pit, he was even more uncomfortable about describing the tattered underwear which was all the clothing that he and his mates could bear on account of the heat. He should have seen then next one coming but he didn't and he was not prepared when she asked him what they did about going to the toilet. 'We do it in what we call the waste, the worked-out area behind us,' came his embarrassed reply.

For the remainder of the evening and for the first time since Tony had known her, Claire's conversation was muted. He knew enough about her to know that she was no snob, but he also knew that one unguarded reply had revealed the gulf between his life and hers. Trying to hide his agitation, he arranged to meet her the following week but, as he half-expected, she did not turn up. He knew that their relationship was at an end.

Benny

Benny Green, in common with most miners, liked his pint; in fact, he liked several pints. But Benny's wife, Martha, frowned on his drinking. Benny always knew, the moment he got home, whether his detour via the working men's club had been detected, by the intensity of the scowl on Martha's face. In fact, it was rarely that her face was not clouded by a scowl to some degree, but the scowl reserved to show her disapproval of Benny's drinking was unmistakeable and would be followed, as sure as night follows day, by a tongue lashing. Benny hated the scowl more than he hated the scolding and he would go to extraordinary lengths to conceal his visits to the club. They were usually short visits, either on his way home from work or his allotment, or on the pretext of going to see one of his pals; but Benny could sink a lot of beer in a short time. The result of all this subterfuge was that Benny usually wore a furtive expression. Even when he had had his fill and was at his most relaxed, he was always on his guard. Between his arduous work at the coal face and the obstacles in the way of his chief source of pleasure, Benny's life could not be described as a happy one.

Martha had 'married beneath her'. Her father was a colliery clerk and a Methodist lay-preacher. Martha greatly admired her father and had hoped to marry someone like him. But she had reached her mid-twenties with nobody suitable in view and when Benny, who was earning good money at the coal face, started paying attention to her, she decided that she had better take what she could get before it was too late. Martha was not what could be described as pretty, but she had an eye-catching figure and a quiet dignity that commanded admiration.

Benny was a short, thick-set lad, but he had a handsome, open face, a ready smile and a sharp wit. His stocky, muscular physique made him the best hewer on his shift and his earnings were seldom surpassed. He had enjoyed easy-going relationships with several girls, all of whom had shown him warmth and affection, but the majestic manner of Martha Davis attracted him and, with due reluctance, she eventually agreed to marry him. Martha did not want to live in a colliery house, so they rented one from a private landlord in a 'respectable' street of the old village. Benny cultivated an allotment whilst Martha kept the tiny front garden of their terraced house trim. With his generous allowance of concessionary coal, Benny was able to keep the boiler of his greenhouse stoked night and day during the cold months, with the result that they enjoyed freshly-picked tomatoes from early June and beautiful chrysanthemum blooms until well after Christmas.

Martha had one baby, a girl, in the third year of their marriage, after which she instituted a contraceptive regime that involved a severe curtailment of Benny's privileges. Their daughter, Janet, was pretty, intelligent and full of life. At the age of eleven, she won a Council scholarship to the grammar school. She left school at sixteen with good grades in her School Certificate and took a job in the office of a wholesale warehouse in the town. Janet loved her father and respected her mother, but she was determined to lead a different life from theirs. She dressed well and made the most of her appearance. She had a wide circle of friends and went out most evenings. To the delight of her mother and the disquiet of her father, a stylish, older man, obviously wealthy, began calling for her and soon his beautiful sports saloon was frequently to be seen at their door. Janet began spending weekends away with him in expensive hotels at fashionable resorts. Benny worried about this much more than Martha did. But it all came to a sudden end. Janet found herself pregnant and her boy-friend confessed to having a wife and child. He chose to remain with his family, but supported Janet financially and she moved to the Midlands to start a new life. Benny and Martha were grieved by what had happened, as any parents would be, but, in Benny, the grief went deeper. He became morose. Not even his visits to the club could cheer him. The only happiness he now had was the brief and infrequent visits of his daughter and grandson.

In the winter of 1930-31, at the age of fifty-nine, Benny caught influenza. Although his physique was still good, his lungs had been damaged by forty years of cigarettes and mine dust and he developed pneumonia. He did his best to conceal the severity of his illness, but one afternoon, as he attempted to take the ashes out, he collapsed. Martha ran to the telephone, at the corner shop, to call an ambulance and he was rushed to hospital. But, within three days, Benny was dead. He was buried in the village cemetery in early February, as the snow began to turn to slush. Three days later the river, swollen by melting snow, overflowed its banks and flooded the village. The low-lying cemetery was the worst hit and the top of Benny's new gravestone was barely visible above three feet of water. Accustomed to periodic flooding, the Council kept a number of large rowboats to provide an emergency service to marooned villagers. On a darkening February afternoon, two Council workmen were rowing through the cemetery on their way back to the depot. One of them, a neighbour and friend of Benny's, who had been at his funeral only a few days previously, nodded towards the submerged grave, looked at his mate in the other end of the boat and reflected: 'Well, at least old Benny is getting as much as he can sup now.'

'Aye, and in peace,' replied his mate.

Togetherness

The Wilsons and the Masons lived in adjacent Council houses at the corner of the street, the Wilsons facing south and the Masons west. A consequence of living on a corner was that each house had a larger than normal front garden, but very little back yard. In fact, the small triangle of land beyond their back doors was not big enough for two lavatories so they had to share one and, even then, it was extremely narrow. This configuration is important to the story.

Edith Wilson was a tall, thin woman with sharp features. She was in her late thirties. She always appeared harassed, an impression that was accentuated by her pale, drawn face and untidy hair. Edith's harassment was probably attributable to her two unruly daughters and a lack of support from her husband. Eric Wilson was rarely seen around the family home. He was a thick-set, coarse featured, prematurely balding man, but always immaculately dressed. He was five years or so older than his wife. He had been paid off from the pit following an accident which had left him with a pronounced limp. Eric was ostensibly a chauffeur for a wealthy business family in the town, but mystery surrounded his comings and goings. On the few occasions when he spent a night at home, he usually arrived after dark and left early the following morning. He was rarely seen in the same car twice and invariably parked whatever vehicle he was driving, several streets away from his home. Rumour had it that he was an underworld enforcer, who had served more than one prison sentence.

The Wilsons had two daughters, Joan being about two years older than her sister, Doreen. Although they had, to some extent, inherited their father's coarse features, they were well-made and not unattractive. With an absentee father and an inadequate mother it is, perhaps, not surprising that the two girls ran wild. They stole from shops and roamed the countryside with boys, raiding gardens, orchards and crops in the fields. The girls were also sexually precocious; by the time they were sixteen and fourteen respectively, they had instructed a whole generation of village boys in female physiology, often accompanied by practical demonstrations, as a result of which they were no longer virgins.

Arthur Mason was a big, muscular man in his fifties. He was showy, vain and a womaniser. He delighted in being the centre of attention and, in order to impress his audience, he often strayed from the truth. Arthur was a shot firer on good pay, but he also moonlighted as a bookmaker's runner, which allowed him to buy flashy clothes and to spend lavishly in the pub. Arthur's wife, Ethel, had no illusions about her husband, but he was a good provider and her main concern was for her family; she had two boys, Frank aged nineteen and Vince seventeen, both of whom were unemployed. There were also other reasons why Ethel did not want to rock the boat: there was her discreet romance with a widower in the town, which she cherished and there was the family betting business which bound her, Arthur and the boys together. Ready-money betting was strictly illegal, but it was the only way for a working man to have a flutter. Since a constant stream of punters to a bookmakers premises would attract the attention of the police, the only way he could operate was to have a team of 'runners' who took bets discreetly, either in pubs and clubs or in their own homes; Arthur was one of them.

Taking bets in the home meant at least one member of the family being available on all racing days, which was almost every day of the week other than Sunday. Since Arthur was a full-time miner, he could only attend to the betting business as his shifts allowed. All the family had to play their part. Their lives revolved around the 'clock' which was collected from the bookmaker early each morning and returned after the last race. A clock-operated locking mechanism was set in a strong steel case, which had a slot for each race of the day. The client's betting slips and money were placed in a leather bag of which there was one for each race. Each bag had a steel rim and immediately before the start of a race, the rim of the bag containing the bets on that race was inserted into the appropriate slot and was automatically locked shut by the clock. It could only be opened by the bookie with his special key. The purpose of the clock was, of course, to prevent dishonesty by the runner, either by placing bets of his own, after the race was run, or by siphoning off losing bets. Winnings were collected by the runner each evening and paid out to the punters as they called. The whole procedure had to be carried out discreetly in order not to attract attention; that is why the whole family was involved. Ethel and her sons took turns in collecting and returning the clock and collecting the winnings. They took different routes and carried the clock in a variety of different bags. The boys, as often as not, would cycle with the clock in their saddle bags. Caution had to be exercised by clients in approaching the Mason's home. Neighbours were bribed to allow punters to gain access via their back yards and openings in walls and fences were made for that purpose.

The Mason's regular clients were a mixed lot. They were mostly male of course; most women who fancied a flutter would send their husbands or male relatives. Sometimes children would be entrusted with the errand, but the Masons discouraged this and experience had taught them never to pay out winnings to children. Most of the punters were moderate backers to whom a shilling a day on the horses was a way of life and who never staked more than they could afford to lose. Most women would only have the odd bet on a big race as a way of marking the occasion. But some men were compulsive gamblers, who were prepared to put the welfare of their families at risk in their pursuit of a big win. The Masons could not help noticing that such men often had distinctive personal characteristics: Les Potts had a perpetual, almost silent cough; Peter Robinson had a twitch which affected the left side of his face and neck, whist Bob Jordan rarely took his hands out of his trouser pockets, where they were continuously engaged in manipulating his genitals: he was known among his acquaintances as 'the pocket billiards champion'.

Edith Wilson did not much like living next door to a bookie's runner, but what upset her more was the shared lavatory. When she first moved into the house and learned of the toilet arrangements, she willingly did her share of the cleaning and sanitising, but she soon found that Ethel Mason was too busy taking bets to reciprocate, despite the fact that the Masons and their clients used the facility much more than she and her two girls did. What offended her most was the toilet paper situation. In the early days, Edith would carefully cut a newspaper into conveniently sized squares, bore a hole in one corner of the wad with a skewer and hang it on a nail in the lavatory wall within reach of the pedestal. But this refinement was too much of a chore for the Masons, who were content to leave yesterday's *Daily Mirror* on the privy floor. Worse still, if the tabloid contained anything of more than passing interest, especially a racing article, it was placed in the kitchen cupboard and didn't reach the lavatory. On days when the preservation of racing history took priority over sanitary needs, Edith became annoyed about the rate at which the cut paper that she supplied disappeared. Eventually she began to keep it on a nail inside her own back door and made sure that her girls followed her example by taking a few sheets whenever they went to the toilet. Occasionally, to register her disapproval, she would give the place a fresh coat of whitewash.

As explained earlier, the shared lavatory was very narrow, its shape dictated by the geometry of the street corner. The door was in the side wall at the remote end from the pedestal and on the adjacent end wall was a shelf on which a candleholder could be placed. It was therefore convenient, at night, to enter, place one's candle on the shelf and walk backwards to the pedestal, baring ones bottom on the way. One winter's evening, Vince, the younger of the Mason boys, then about seventeen, was sitting on the lavatory, in total darkness, thinking about girls, when Joan, the elder of the Wilson sisters, opened the door. Vince remained silent as Joan placed her candle on the shelf and, oblivious of his presence, slowly reversed towards him, lowering her knickers and lifting her skirt as she went.

Mother's Boy

Desmond Roberts was an only child. His father, Les, was a deputy at the pit, whilst his mother, Gladys, took in sewing and was a pillar of the local branch of the Co-operative Women's Guild. With the help of the Co-op Building Society, the Roberts were buying their own house in a small development of two-bedroomed semi's on the edge of the village. On the day that Desmond was born and pronounced strong and healthy, Gladys decided that one child was enough to bring up properly and she severely curtailed Les' connubial privileges; they were never fully restored.

Baby Desmond had the most beautiful high pram that the village had ever seen. As a toddler, he was never known to have dirty knees or a speck on his clothes. As a schoolboy, he had the smartest suit and the cleanest shirt of any boy in the playground. With his mother's coaching, he was always top of his class. He went to Sunday school at the village Methodist Chapel, immaculately dressed, every Sunday morning and afternoon. He was given sixpence pocket money every Friday, but he had to account to his mother for what he had spent it on. At the age of eleven, Desmond won a Council scholarship to the grammar school in the town, where he continued to stand out among his classmates. He did his homework conscientiously every evening, after which he was allowed out to play, but only for an hour; he had to be in by eight o'clock and in bed by nine.

But from a very early age, Desmond began to rebel against his parent's strict control. His revolt began during his first year at school when his contact with other children brought the realisation that his life was not like theirs. He began to pick up their language, which was largely a mixture of colloquial expressions, slang words and expletives. Of course, he never attempted to use his new powers of expression at home. He started to steal money, not from his mother, who knew the contents of her purse down to the last ha'penny, but from his father who was far less careful and never knew to a shilling or two how much change he had in his pockets. There were also occasional visitors who went away slightly poorer than when they arrived. This supplement to Desmond's income allowed him to indulge himself with all the sweets and ice-cream that he could eat and to treat his friends as well.

At grammar school, under the influence of other boys, Desmond began to smoke. A number of the boys would gather behind the bicycle shed at playtime and light up. Of course, he had to be careful that he did not go home with any hint of smoke on his breath or trace of nicotine on his hands, so he kept a bottle of mouthwash in his desk and carefully rubbed his stained fingers along convenient wall coping stones on his way home from school.

Inevitably, at around thirteen, Desmond began to develop a lively interest in girls. He did not have much opportunity to pursue his new interest at school because, although the school was co-educational, the girls tended to keep to themselves in small cliques and treated the boys with apparent disdain. But around this time Desmond's parents relaxed their control to the extent of allowing him to go to the cinema on one evening a week and on Saturday afternoons. It had to be the early evening show and he had to be home by nine, but he could always be sure of meeting a few of his friends there. The back stalls were popular with teenagers of both sexes, eager to exploit the darkness and the closeness of the seats to make overtures that they would never have dared to make under any other circumstances.

With the social skills that he learned in the cinema, Desmond was able to make an even more important discovery. He had discerned that the girls in his group at Sunday school were somewhat naïve compared to the more streetwise girls he met in the cinema and, armed with this knowledge, he was able, on most Sunday afternoons, to persuade one or other of them to walk home with him along the country lane which skirted the village, rather than taking the direct route along the high street. He knew all the secluded spots along the way and, pausing at one of them, he would take advantage of his companion's naïvety and his own back-stalls skills to take liberties with her. He never went too far, because he knew that the consequences could be disastrous, but he was skilful and patient enough to make it a mutually rewarding experience, with no recriminations. The result was that there were few Sunday afternoons when he did not have a willing companion to walk home with.

At eighteen, Desmond shone in the Higher School Certificate examinations and was accepted into one of the northern universities to study medicine. For the first time in his life he found himself beyond his mother's control and he took full advantage of his freedom. He soon made friends with other students who were as determined as he to enjoy the social advantages of university life and almost every evening a group of them were to be found in cafés, bars, dance halls or wherever the opportunity to drink, smoke and chat up young women presented itself. The local girls were no shrinking violets and many of them considered it a feather in their cap to be seen hanging on the arm of a medical student. Besides, if the worst came to the worst and they fell pregnant, 'he would know what to do about it wouldn't he'? In this they were not wrong. Abortion procedure, although years ahead in the MB curriculum, was passed from generation to generation of first-year students and the implements were readily available. Desmond knew exactly what to do if his current girl-friend should miss a period.

But if his grasp of abortion procedure was precocious, the same could not be said of Desmond's proper studies. Bright though he was, his nights out and the time he needed for recovery on the mornings after, took their toll of his work. He had done well at school because he was able to grasp the basic principles on which subjects like maths and physics depended. But medicine was not like that; it involved the absorption of large volumes of narrative and that required time – time which Desmond's extra-curricula activities did not leave him. He knew that he would not pass his first-year examinations, so he dropped out on the day that they started.

Desmond did not go home because he was not ready to face his mother's recriminations. But he was fortunate enough to find an elderly widow who was prepared to take him in as a lodger. Of course, he had to get a job, but what? What could a twenty-year old, failed medical student do? Most potential employers who interviewed him were impressed with his obvious intelligence, but sceptical about the dependability of someone who had dropped out of university. Desmond was determined not to follow his father down the pit and the only other job offered to him was that of door-to-door representative of a loan company. The job involved collecting weekly repayments on existing loans and agreeing new loans where the prospective client was judged to be credit-worthy - a 'tally man'. It was a waste of Desmond's education, but it offered a basic wage sufficient to get by on and good commission on new loans, so he took it.

But it was like putting an alcoholic in charge of a distillery. Most of the clients were young housewives, struggling to make ends meet. Frequently, Desmond would find himself faced with some young woman, pleading for a loan which he doubted she could pay back or asking for a week's repayment to be deferred. What was he to do when a client in this situation made herself particularly attractive and hinted that there were alternative ways of repaying the debt? Desmond was soon having sex frequently with several of his clients and, of course, making good their missed repayments out of his own wages. Inevitably, one of these women fell pregnant. She already had two children and didn't want any more. She was fairly sure that Desmond was the father and she was worried that, if she had the child, it would be obvious, in some way or other, that it was not her husband's. When she confided her fears to Desmond, he told her not to worry. On his next visit he arrived early, equipped with the instruments he had acquired illegally at medical school. Late that evening, his patient, weak and ill, flushed a small object down the toilet. She would never again miss a weekly repayment.

When a similar situation arose with another client, it ended very differently. The woman had made it clear to Desmond that she was unhappily married and wanted him. When she became pregnant, she wanted to leave her husband and live with Desmond. He was not particularly fond of her and, promising that they would be together when the time was right, persuaded her to have an abortion. When, in the course of the following months, Desmond showed no sign of wanting to set up home with her, the woman began to put more and more pressure on him. Eventually she went to the police and accused him of carrying out an abortion on her.

Desmond was arrested, charged with a breach of the Offences Against the Person Act and remanded on bail. As the date set for his trial approached, Desmond began to realise that he would, in all probability, go to prison. He accepted that it was no more than his reckless way of life had merited. But prison held no terrors for him comparable to that of facing his mother, after she had read the newspaper accounts of his trial.

Double Grief

It was an hour into the morning shift when the overman warned that there was gas about. Seconds later there was a blinding flash, a deafening roar and a blast of searing hot air; props and struts flew and an avalanche of rock came down. When the pit had been evacuated, five men had not emerged and the rescue team went in.

Alice Morgan could not force herself to look closely at the bundle of broken bones and torn flesh that she was being asked to confirm had been her husband, Bob. Only two of the five missing men had so far been found, but the body of Bob's mate, Alf, had already identified by his wife and they were pulled out together, so this one must be Bob, mustn't it? She nodded an uncertain 'yes' and, blinded by tears, stumbled away.

At the time of Bob's funeral, a week later, three men were still unaccounted for and the minds of the mourners were as much on them as they were on Bob. The rescue work was slow and back-breaking. Ton after ton of rock had to be broken out, passed back and stacked by hand to support the roof as they drove forward. Relays of rescuers toiled night and day, long after all hope of finding anyone alive had been abandoned. In the course of the next ten days, the three men were located, one by one, brought to the surface and examined for identifying signs. One of them was Bob! His face was, with difficulty, still recognisable and his distinctive belt was still around his waist. There was no problem in naming the remaining two, leaving the one who had been mistakenly buried in Bob's name to be identified by elimination.

Alice was still in shock from her first ordeal and ill-prepared for a second. It left her numb and confused. Relatives and friends had to step in to help her through it. On a raw March day, Alice Morgan, dazed and bewildered, followed her husband's coffin for the second time in a month.

The Parkin Gang

George Parkin and his gang reigned in terror over the village and the surrounding countryside throughout the 1930s. The gang consisted of about two dozen young men in their late teens or early twenties; some of them, like George, were unemployed and were full-time gang members, whilst others were miners whose availability for gang activities was determined by their pattern of shift work. George was a tall, powerfully-built chap with a cruel streak. He had developed a taste for power through bullying other children at school; an offence which the teachers did nothing to check. He was a mild epileptic and his domineering attitude to others may have been intended, consciously or otherwise, to compensate for what he perceived as a personal weakness. His condition may also have had something to do with the teachers' reluctance to confront him about his behaviour. His indulgent parents, perpetually anxious about his health, had failed to exercise any discipline and, although he never abused them, he permitted them little influence over his life. George's fits caused frequent absences from school, as a result of which his educational progress was poor and he left school scarcely able to read or write. He was virtually unemployable and the 'dole' queue inevitably acquainted him with others who had time on their hands.

For all his personal defects, George knew how to lead. He took full advantage of his size and strength and his domineering personality to exact loyalty and obedience from the members of his gang. He also knew how to delegate; he had a deputy who could take charge in his absence and who, being much more of a thinker than George, came up with most of the ideas underlying the gang's activities. George also recognised two or three lieutenants who could lead small groups when projects required the gang to be split up.

The gang met most mornings in a derelict farm building on the edge of the old part of the village. There they would decide how they were going to

19

spend the day. Weather permitting, they would usually forage around the countryside helping themselves from crops of potatoes, carrots, peas, beans or whatever was in season. Those with air guns or catapults would attempt to shoot rabbits or ducks. There were usually snares to empty. Failing all else, someone would peg discarded stockings over several entrances to a rabbit warren, throw a handful of calcium carbide down one of the holes, urinate on it and, when sufficient acetylene had been generated, throw a lighted match into the hole. The resulting explosion would panic the rabbits, some of which would be caught in the stockings as they bolted. The gang did these things quite openly because nobody dared challenge them; a group of twenty or more aggressive young men was an intimidating sight and no landowner could confront them. As long as there was no outright criminality the police did not intervene. Besides, in addition to the odd air gun and catapult, they were all armed. Each member of the gang had a leather strap looped around his shoulder, under his jacket, with the loose end hanging down inside his sleeve. The strap terminated in a heavy weight, usually a large nut and bolt with the end of the strap pinched between them and the bolt sawn off short. With a barely perceptible movement, the loop of the strap could be slipped off the shoulder, down the arm and grasped in the hand, leaving a compact, heavy weight swinging on twelve inches of leather strap, which could be wielded with frightening force. The very sight of these weapons, produced simultaneously and unexpectedly by a score of hostile young men, was enough to quell any opposition and it is doubtful whether the weapons were ever used in anger.

Having spent the morning marauding the countryside, the gang would return to their headquarters in the barn, light a fire, cook their stolen food and spend a leisurely afternoon eating, talking about girls and sex, and making plans for the days ahead. On warm summer days they would not return to the building, but would light a fire in the corner of a field, cook their food and sit around in a circle doing whatever they would have done in the barn. Although they were invariably trespassing, they made no attempt at concealment, since no-one dared approach them. People out for a walk, having seen them, would make a lengthy detour to avoid them.

As the years passed, members came and went: some to work in other areas, some to get married, some to go to jail, but with George at its head, the size and nature of the gang changed little until the appearance of a remarkable new recruit. Jean Dixon was a young woman of about eighteen and as hard as nails. She came from a large family and had received little care or attention from her parents other than an occasional clip around the ear. Her ragged and unwashed appearance had brought derision on her at school and she had retaliated by becoming a rebel and a bully. As a teenager, Jean was not unattractive with pleasant facial features and a large, shapely figure, but her confrontational nature gained her few friends and her rejection of authority meant that she never kept a job for long. Girls were afraid of her and because of her reputation, most of them were forbidden by their parents to have anything to do with her. Boys were intimidated by her; she bullied one or two of them into having sex with her and then humiliated them by criticising their performance.

Jean, like almost everyone else in the village, was aware of the Parkin gang. She often saw them emerging from the barn in a morning and returning in the afternoon. She would sometimes see the smoke from a fire in the corner of a field and knew that the gang would be squatting around it. She wondered what they did and what it would be like to be with them and have a share in it. She stopped George Parkin in the street one day and asked him what they did. When George tried to brush her off, she became more insistent, finally asking him if she could join the gang. George told her not to be ridiculous and walked away. But Jean was warming to the idea and would not be put off. She started pestering George every time she saw him. When he pointed out that the things they did were not suitable for girls, she replied that girl's things didn't interest her. He said that she would be a liability if they got into a fight; she replied that she could probably teach some of the gang about fighting. When she made it clear that sexual favours would be available to gang members, George knew that there was no use arguing any longer; he would have a revolt on his hands if it became known that he had refused such an offer. He talked it over with the gang who, of course, were all in favour and Jean joined them a few days later.

Jean entered enthusiastically into the gang spirit; she did her share of the chores around the barn but resisted any suggestion that housekeeping was her rôle. She went out with the gang on every expedition and proved as resourceful and reliable as any of them. When it came to sex, she soon learned that she had to be available to any member, any time and anywhere. If she had thought that she would receive any consideration or respect, she was mistaken. Whether it was in the barn, in a field or in a wood, whoever wanted her took her, roughly and greedily, with other members looking on and waiting for their turn. In the fields they would gather round in a circle to shield the proceedings from prying eyes and to shout encouragement. For most members, it was just sex and there was no sentiment or solicitude.

Inevitably, Jean became pregnant. She did her best to conceal it from the gang until there was no denying it. When George asked her what she was going to do about it, she said she didn't know. She knew that her family

21

would be no help and that she would have to fend for herself. George asked her if she wanted to get married.

'I suppose so' she replied, 'but who would have me with a baby on the way and nobody knowing the father?'

'Who would you want if you could have your pick of the gang?' asked George. The only member of the gang who had ever shown Jean any respect as a person was Nick Green, and his name came to her lips. Nick was an easy-going, soft-hearted sort of a chap and George decided to lean on him; he wanted this business cleared up before people began asking questions. That afternoon, he called Nick to one side. 'It's time you were married, Nick' he said abruptly.

'Don't you think that's something for me to decide?' asked Nick.

George told Nick what the situation was and said that he was the one that Jean wanted. He did not want any officials poking their noses into the affairs of the gang, so the two of them were to leave and set up home together.

'So get courting,' said George, menacingly.

Nick thought it over. He had a soft spot for Jean and he could do worse; at least with her his sex life would never be dull. He was twenty-five and as ready for marriage as he ever would be, but he did not want the other gang members thinking that they could continue their association with her if he married her. He spelled out this condition to George, who promised that there would be no problems of that sort.

Nick and Jean were married on an autumn day in 1935, while her condition could still be obscured by her coat. They got the tenancy of a colliery house and Jean did her best to be a good wife. She had a baby boy, who, as he grew up, was not readily identifiable with any particular member of the gang. He was followed by two sisters and a brother, each of whom had their father's features. On the surface they appeared to be a tolerably happy family, but whether Nick Green was ever able to erase from his memory the image of his wife, copulating daily with assorted members of the Parkin gang, only he knew.

They Were Not Divided

In 1934, the village football team won the South Yorkshire amateur league championship. On the Saturday following the final, the team members were carried on the shoulders of their supporters, from the workmen's club to the miner's welfare hall for a Council reception and tea. Nobody enjoyed themselves better or more deservedly than striker, Alan Bennet, winger, Peter Wright and defender, George Ogden. Alan had scored the first of the two winning goals; Peter had 'made' both goals by his accurate shots to the strikers, whilst George had helped to fend off every attack by the opposing team.

Alan was a single chap in his early twenties: handsome, athletic and a good mixer. He knew several attractive girls, but was not yet ready to settle down and skilfully steered clear of any serious commitment. He was an only child and was spoiled by his parents, with whom he still lived. Other than paying for his keep, he was not expected to do anything around the house and consequently had a lot of leisure time.

Peter was also single, a few months short of his twentieth birthday and a bit on the shy side, especially where girls were concerned. He had two older, married brothers and, as the only son left at home, felt it his duty to do what he could to help his ageing parents. He looked what he was: an intelligent, thoughtful young man; if better educational opportunities had been open to him he would have been unlikely to go down the pit. His great love was fishing and whenever his work and his footballing commitments permitted, he would cycle to his favourite spot on the river with his rod tied to the crossbar of his bicycle and his haversack on his back.

George was almost thirty and a happily married man with two small children. He was a big strong fellow, who was proud of being a miner and of the money he earned, which enabled him to provide well for his family. His wife was also his friend, a wonderful mother to his children and a diligent housekeeper; George's work and his football were the only things that took him out of her sight.

The three friends were not only team mates but workmates as well, who worked on the same coal face and spent five shifts a week within sight of each other. Their mutual support of each other at work and their day to day chatter drew them close together and there was little about any of them that the other two did not know and understand. Their families too knew and respected each other.

A few days after the celebration of their team's victory, the friendship of the three men, their football, their work and their lives came to an abrupt end. An unpredicted fault above the coalface placed unsustainable pressure on the props and the roof came down on them. It took the rescue team two days to get them out.

Because of their close association, the men's families decided that it would be appropriate to have a joint funeral. The cortèges from the three homes assembled outside the Welfare Hall and drove in procession to the Methodist Chapel. Members of the football team and other friends volunteered as pallbearers. For the second time in less than a month, the village witnessed the three friends borne aloft on the shoulders of their comrades.

To Be a Farmer's Boy

It was man's God-given instinct to subdue and herd animals that enabled him to emerge from the hunter-gatherer stage and settle the land. That instinct showed itself in some of the village boys by their readiness to walk miles, without any hope of reward, for the opportunity to wield a stick and guide a few cows, sheep or goats from one place to another. Farmers in the surrounding countryside usually welcomed this free help in bringing cows in for milking or in moving their herds from pasture to pasture. Likewise, those selling livestock at the town's cattle market would often appreciate help in transferring their animals from the pens to the auction ring or from the ring to the buyers transport. Any Saturday or Sunday would find eager youngsters, armed with ash saplings, hanging around farm gates, waiting to be asked to give a hand. Similarly, on market days, the back seats of the auction ring would be occupied by truants from school, eager to help in moving livestock around and hoping for that rare occasion when they would be given the chance to lead an animal around the ring as the bids were made. It seemed that miner's sons, knowing what the future held for them, found this type of pastoral activity particularly appealing and what a country boy would regard as labour, they considered a privilege.

Brothers Norman and George Pearson were small dairy farmers, who took full advantage of this pool of free labour. They kept cows in fields a little way out of the village, but for some reason, perhaps connected with water and electricity supplies, their barn, milking sheds and dairy were located a quarter of a mile away on the edge of the built-up area. Their herd, therefore, had to be coaxed along the lane from the fields to the sheds, hand-milked, and driven back again, except in winter, when they remained undercover.

The Pearson brothers were the sons of a miner, who had been killed in a pit accident in the 1920s when they were in their late teens. Their father had been a hard man who, perhaps to prepare them for a miner's life, had

25

treated them quite harshly. The result was that the boys grew up closely attached to their mother, who tried to make up for their father's roughness and was determined that they would not go down the mine. When Mrs. Pearson received the compensation for her husband's death, she looked around for some way of investing the money that would provide her sons, still living with her, with secure and congenial employment. It so happened that a small dairy farm, close to the village, had been hit by an outbreak of foot and mouth disease and the herd had been slaughtered by government order. The elderly owner did not have the heart to start afresh, so the fields and buildings were put on the market at a knock-down price. Mrs. Pearson snapped up the property and, following the statutory disinfection procedure, restocked the farm and handed it over to her sons.

Because the dairy had been out of business for several months, its customers had been lost, mainly to the Co-op. But in attempting to win back the trade, the Pearsons had one big advantage: their labour costs were virtually nil. There were boys in the village who were not only happy to herd their cows for them but, for that privilege, were prepared to deliver milk without payment too. Delivery was by horse and cart and commenced each morning at six o'clock. Every morning, school or no school, would see two or three youngsters waiting at the dairy gate for the cart to emerge. There was no bottling and no pasteurising. The milk was loaded onto the cart in churns and decanted into buckets, which were taken to the customer's doors by the boys and from which they would ladle out the required quantities into the customer's jugs, using tin measuring cans. Considering the inconvenience and the lack of hygiene inherent in this process, it was a wonder that the Pearsons ever won back their market or, for that matter, how they avoided spreading all sorts of infections around the village. A boy could be tending to the horse one minute and ladling out milk the next. But, it must be admitted, the milk was deliciously rich and creamy and, above all, because it cost the Pearsons little or nothing to deliver, they were able to undercut their competitors. It only took one of them to supervise the delivery and drive the cart while the other attended to the herd and the dairy, assisted by his small army of willing helpers.

Inevitably, a hierarchy developed among the unpaid volunteers, in which the longer-serving or more reliable boys rose to the top. It was soon observed, by the newer recruits, that the older boys spent less and less time delivering milk or herding cows. Instead, they seemed to find more and more to do in the barn, under the personal supervision of one or both of the Pearson brothers. Some of the more inquisitive boys began to ask questions about what took place in the barn, but they only met with evasive answers and hints that they might find out some day, if they stayed around long enough. Peering through the windows revealed nothing because the glass was grimy and the light inside dim. Those who had the audacity to try the doors found them barred on the inside. Eventually, gossip leaked out into the village about mysterious goings-on at the farm and parents, who had been happy for their sons to have a healthy outdoor interest, were no longer so sure and began to keep them away. But the Pearson brothers were never entirely without help, for they had made a remarkable discovery: that some boys will do almost anything for the privilege of herding a few cows.

Mis-spent Youth

As a boy, Cliff Wright was a bit of a disappointment to his family. His father was an overman at the pit and his mother was a pillar of the Methodist chapel; they took pride in their place in the community and had aspirations for their children. Cliff was a tall, well-built boy with pleasant features, but he had no love of learning and he disliked school and all that it stood for. Consequently, when he reached fourteen and it was time to leave school, Cliff was faced with a very limited choice of occupations. His elder brother was a promising police constable whilst his sister had progressed from salesgirl to assistant buyer in the town's only department store, but jobs like that required ambition and dedication and were not for Cliff. When he eventually decided to go down the pit, it came as a blow to his parents, but mining had advantages for Cliff. All that it asked of him was hard manual work which, with his physique and stamina, was no problem to him. It made no intellectual demands on him, whilst the shift system afforded him plenty of time to indulge his one passion: snooker. Also his relatively good pay allowed him to spend as much time as he wished at the tables. The billiard hall, with its relaxed atmosphere and easy sociability, suited Cliff's personality. More importantly, it turned out that he had the aptitude for judging angles and distances, superb eyesight and the precise control over his movements that are essential to the game. It was not long before Cliff could outplay all the regulars at his local hall and within a couple of years, he was winning regional competitions. His name began to be mentioned as a possible contender in the national championships.

On a black day in 1928, almost at the end of his shift, Cliff was caught in a fall of rock. It was only a minor fall and Cliff was soon pulled out, but an examination in 'casualty' showed that he had suffered multiple injuries including a severely damaged hip and a shattered right hand, his 'cue' hand.. Weeks in hospital and months of outpatient treatment followed. The enforced idleness and the realisation that he would never again play top-level snooker produced a black depression, which a fortnight at a miner's convalescent home on the Yorkshire coast did little to lift.

The wheels of the miner's compensation machinery ground slowly and after a long wait, Cliff received a 'full and final' settlement. It was not a fortune and was certainly not adequate recompense for his injuries and loss of employment but, he thought, it might just be enough to buy a corner shop or a small pub, which would afford him a living and keep him occupied.

Cliff spent months scanning the classified advertisements in the newspapers and limping around the streets looking for 'for sale' signs. Each prospect he investigated proved to be either beyond his means or unsuitable for some reason or other. In his wanderings he usually avoided the billiard hall, because the memory of what had been taken away from him was still too painful. One day he found himself passing the door of the hall and he was astonished to find it closed with an estate agent's 'for sale' sign pasted over it.. As he walked home, Cliff wondered why the hall had closed and whether it would ever reopen. The idea didn't hit him immediately, but it slowly dawned on him that, if he could only afford it, here was an opportunity to combine his abiding interest in snooker with a job and, who knows? perhaps even a decent living. The hours would be long, because billiard halls were expected to open mid-morning and to close when the last customers went home, but Cliff was not going anywhere and had no wife or family to consider.

The closure of the hall turned out to be due to the illness of the previous proprietor. The asking price proved to be more than Cliff's assets but, with his compensation money deposited in the local bank, he had no difficulty in obtaining an interview with the manager. Cliff knew nothing about business planning, but his knowledge of the billiard hall business that he had gathered as customer, together with copies of past accounts supplied by the vendor, enabled the bank manager to form a favourable view of his prospects and to offer him a loan sufficient to cover the shortfall and to provide some working capital. The hall itself was on a suitably long lease.

And so, Cliff found himself once more spending his days in the old familiar surroundings, but this time as proprietor and not as a punter. He savoured once more the smoke-laden atmosphere, the sight of the tables, each in its own pool of light, the little dramas unfolding on the green baize and the non-stop, male banter. He became the confidant of some of his regulars: someone who could be depended upon to lend a sympathetic ear to their triumphs and tragedies.

The business did well enough to enable Cliff to meet his repayments to the bank and, when the loan was paid off, he began to accumulate capital.

He heard of a hall in a neighbouring mining village which had run into difficulties due to poor management. Cliff went to look at it and quickly saw how an injection of capital and his own style of management could soon turn it around. Drawing on his good standing with the bank, he raised another loan, bought his second hall and appointed, as manager, one of his regular customers, whose good sense and knowledge of the game he had come to respect. He also hired an under-manager to work between the two halls in order to give himself and the other manager some time off.

Cliff had always had an eye for the girls and, before his accident, had never been short of female company. His injuries and the demands of establishing his business had resulted in a hermit-like existence for several years, but with the income from two halls and as much free time as he now chose to take, he began to think of marriage and family life. He often received invitations to weddings, christenings and parties from his friends and customers; now, instead of automatically declining them, he began accepting them occasionally and paying more attention to his social life. Eventually, he renewed the acquaintance of an old girlfriend who, in the meantime had been married and divorced. The two of them rediscovered a mutual attraction and it was not long before Cliff found himself married and raising a family in a smart, modern 'semi' on a new housing estate.

The acquisition of his second billiard hall gave Cliff a taste for expansion and, in the course of the next ten years, he bought out the remaining three which lay within the area that he thought he could comfortably cover. He did not drive on account of his injuries and was dependant upon public transport and taxis. He got into the habit of staying overnight when he visited his satellite halls, in order to ensure that they were being properly run at all hours.

Cliff was now becoming a wealthy man. He bought a large Victorian villa in a leafy suburb of the town and widened his social circle. His business ambitions were given a boost when he heard that the freehold of the whole block which housed his original hall was coming onto the market. It included several shops, a number of offices and a busy café, all bringing in good rents. The fact that Cliff's own premises were leased had always bothered him slightly and here was an opportunity to secure them, whilst, at the same time, making a sound investment and enhancing his standing in the town. He approached the vendors, negotiated what he considered to be a favourable price and, yet again with the support of his bank manager, became landlord of the village's biggest commercial property.

Cliff's enjoyment of his hard-won prosperity was all too short. His years of breathing coal dust in the pit, the debilitating effects of his injuries and the smoke-laden atmosphere in which he had spent so much of his working life, all took their toll and he died in his late fifties. His wife and children were not interested in carrying on the business and everything was to be sold to provide each of them with a substantial inheritance. When the will was read, it made provision for two beneficiaries that his family did not expect. It turned out that Cliff had a long-time partner and a teenage illegitimate son in the village where he had bought his second billiard hall all those years ago.

Harry, Ten Going on Eleven

New Year's Day. Another year, 1936. I will be eleven this year. Went round the houses 'happy new year-ing' this morning with Jeff Godwin; we got five-pence each. Cold these mornings. No snow yet. Good job we have got plenty of coal – best thing about Dad being a miner. Dad banks the fire up with slack before we go to bed and it lasts all night. His greenhouse boiler never goes out all winter. Every month when the coal comes, I help Dad to shovel it into the coal house; he has to put boards across the doorway to hold it all.

Went back to school today; I'm sharing a desk with Nancy Liddel. We are doing long division in maths and John Masefield's poetry in English. I like a poem called *Cargoes*. There is ice on Barton's pond but it is not thick enough to walk on. Walker's dog, Spot, went on and fell through a hole in the ice. Nobody could reach him and he drowned. Somebody said that I had thrown a stick for him to fetch but it was a lie: he was already in the water when I got there. He could not get a grip on the ice to get out and he slowly went under. We all felt bad. Sally Walker and her Mam cried.

I had to take the wireless accumulator to Mr. Chambers to be charged up today. He has rows and rows of them all bubbling away, connected by wires to rows of switches on the wall. He has been doing this since he lost his leg in a pit accident. He says the gas bubbling out of the accumulators is explosive and if you were to strike a match in there it would all go up with a bang. The ice is thick enough to walk on at last. Nobody is going on Barton's pond because of Spot Walker, but we have made a long slide on the railway cutting; it's great!

February. It snowed during the night, about a foot deep. I had to go to school, in my wellies. Everybody was throwing snowballs. I took my sledge to the pit heap after school. It was hard work pulling it up but it was worth it coming down. Jeff Godwin had a go while I had a rest. It is snowing again tonight; it will be really deep tomorrow.

King George, who gave us all a mug last year, when it was his Silver Jubilee, died last night. I wonder where that mug went? We've got a new king now – Edward. Mam says he is very popular and he is going to do something about unemployment and poverty. Dad says he will believe it when it happens. The women are gossiping about who the new king is going to marry.

It was hard walking to school today through a foot and a half of snow; you had to lift your feet up really high. The Council are supposed to clear it but it has usually melted by the time they get around to it. Nancy Liddel didn't get to school today; I expect the snow was too deep for her; she has further to walk than me. Our teacher didn't get in either; she comes by bike from another village. The headmaster took her place. He told us how John Masefield went to sea as a boy, on a sailing ship, all the way to Chile in South America. He showed us the route on the wall map. He read us one of Masefield's poems called *Roadways* and said we should aim to travel and see the world. He wrote the poem on the blackboard and underlined two lines:

'Most roads lead men homeward,
But my road leads me forth.'

He played us a tune to 'Roadways' on the piano and we all sang it.

Listened to Gracie Fields on the wireless last night; she sang *'Sally'* and *'Red Sails in the Sunset'*. She also sang some daft songs but I didn't like them. We always listen to 'Band Wagon' on Wednesday nights and 'Music Hall' on Saturdays. On Sundays the BBC programmes are boring, so we listen to Radio Luxembourg which plays lots of good tunes. They always have an advert for Ovaltine. Jeff Godwin's Mam enrolled us both in the 'Ovaltinies' a few years ago, but we are a bit too big for that now. I've still got the badge.

The snow is thawing fast. The stream at the back of the houses is nearly up to the top of the bank and looks like cocoa. I hope we don't get flooded. Helped Dad in the greenhouse, washing plant pots and seed trays. He is sowing tomato seeds and planting chrysanthemum cuttings. He says if the boiler doesn't go out we shall have the first tomatoes in the village come June.

Today is pancake-day, Shrove Tuesday. I think it is something to do with filling up before fasting for Lent. Nobody filled up better than me. Mam did a stack of pancakes and I put lemon juice and sugar on mine. I lost count of how many I had. Lovely! Everybody took their whips and tops and marbles to school. You had to be careful in the playground not to get hit by somebody's whip. I think whip and top is boring, but I love marbles. I lost a few today, but I will get them back before long. The whip and top craze only lasts a couple of days before everybody gets fed-up with it, but marbles goes on for weeks.

March. Mr. and Mrs. Kelly, who live next door, came rolling home drunk again last night; they do it nearly every Friday and Saturday. You could hear them coming down the street singing *Danny Boy*. As soon as they got into their house you could hear them shouting at one another and then pots and pans and furniture started crashing. I wonder how they feel this morning.

Mam sent me to Ma Schofield's for some teacakes. She is the widow of a miner who got killed in the pit. She makes teacakes to eke out her pension. There's hardly any currents in them; Dad says that before she bakes them, she lines them up at the bottom of her garden and throws currents at them from her back doorstep, one by one.

The close season for fishing starts today so there will be none until the middle of June. It has been too cold and windy to go lately anyway. There are some snowdrops along the hedgerows. I like sitting next to Nancy Liddel. With not having any sisters I didn't know that girls could be nice to talk to.

April. I April-fooled some of my friends this morning but I got caught out myself as well. The marble craze is over and it is now bows and arrows. That is because we've been having Robin Hood stories at school. What a rotter that Sheriff of Nottingham was. There is a place near here called Barnesdale Bar where Robin Hood and his men used to hang out and a well where they used to get their water. I cut a willow stick from down by the stream and Dad helped me to make it into a bow. It should be yew, but there are no yew trees, except in the churchyard in the old village and the vicar wouldn't like us cutting his trees down. My arrows are not much good. Some kids have lashed nails to the tips of theirs but Dad says that is dangerous.

We went to my Auntie Rosie's at Nottingham as usual for Easter. We went by bus. I know the way by heart. Auntie Rosie is my Mam's sister and she is really nice. My Uncle Fred has a sweets and tobacco shop and he always gives me a huge Easter egg with my name on it. My cousin, John, is two years older than me and takes me exploring. When the weather is warm, the lace mills have their windows open and you can see rows and rows of machines, all rattling away and their bobbins spinning round. The mill girls sometimes wave to us. When we went to the castle, I could imagine Robin Hood having a sword fight with that horrid Sheriff. Felt sad when it was time to leave Auntie Rosie's. When we got home, I went to help my Grandad on his allotment. He let me sow some peas and carrot seed. I had to rake the soil really fine. I hope they grow. I love raw peas and carrots.

Got into a fight with Terry Bennet at school. He started calling me names and pushing me backward around the playground for no reason. I was scared at first because he is bigger than me, but then I saw red and flew at him, pounding him with my fists as hard as I could. Nobody really won, but I could tell that he was glad when a teacher parted us. I don't think he will try to bully me again. Havn't told Mam or Dad. We started some new sums about ratios and gradients which I didn't understand, but Nancy Liddel helped me with them. I can do them now.

May. It's getting a lot warmer and there are lots of flowers out. Went to the woods with Jeff Godwin to pick some bluebells. Mam was pleased with them. They smell lovely.

The Council are putting up road crossings where the traffic will have to stop to let people cross. There are two rows of metal studs that you have to walk between and an orange ball on a black and white pole at each side of the road to warn drivers. They call them Belisha Beacons after somebody in the government who thought them up. We have also got rules for crossing the road printed on the back page of our school exercise books. You have to look right, left, then right again to see that the road is clear before crossing.

Mice are getting into the big cupboard that runs along the side of our classroom. Our teacher has started setting a trap and every time it goes off, we take it in turns to take the dead mouse out. We've caught five already and I havn't had my turn yet.

It was the chapel anniversary service last Sunday. All us kids sat on staging on the platform and the adults in the pews. I was near to the top and I could see Nancy Liddel further down. She looked nice. She told me afterwards that her Mam had bought her a new frock and shoes to come in.

June. Hooray! the fishing season has started. I caught a perch in the railway cutting on Saturday but it was only little so I put it back. Early morning is the best time for the big ones.

My Grandad's allotment is near the railway line and we all went last week to see a new engine pass by. It is streamlined and bright silver. It's called *Silver Link*. It was built near here at Doncaster. I'll bet it's good for flattening nails. If you put a long nail on the line before a big engine comes along, it flattens it into a dagger. It also flattens ha'pennies as big as pennies, but they are really thin and don't work penny slot machines or the gas meter. I'd get a belt if Dad knew I went on the railway line.

A big poster has gone up advertising a new sort of holiday place at Skegness, called a holiday camp. Dad says it will be a long time before we can afford to stay there. We sometimes go to Skeggy, but only for a day excursion on the train, organised by Dad's club. Its great though because all the kids get a big bag of sweets and a bottle of pop each and a big red badge with the club's name on it in case we get lost.

Nancy Liddel was off school poorly last week but she is back now. I'm ever so glad she is better. I walked home from school with her as far as the crossroads, where we go in different directions. I got my leg pulled by some of the lads for walking home with a girl, but I don't care.

July. A war has started in Spain. It's called a civil war because both sides belong to the same country. I don't know what it is about, but there is a lot of fighting and the newspapers are full of it. Some men are going from England but I don't know which side they are on.

There was a club excursion to Cleethorpes last Saturday. It was scorching hot but we couldn't get to the sea for ages because the tide was out. It goes out for miles at Cleethorpes and all you can see is ripples in the sand which hurt your bare feet. When the sea came in near enough to paddle it was nearly time to catch the train home. But I had a good time on the fairground with my cousins while our Mams and Dads were in the pub. I bought a smashing sheath knife from Woolworth's for sixpence but I couldn't find it when I got home. I wonder what happened to it.

Jeff Godwin has joined the Boy Scouts and he persuaded me to go with him last night. I didn't like it. It is run by grown men in short trousers. They were ordering us about one minute and playing rough games with us the next. I won't go again. Mam doesn't like the idea because the scout troop is attached to St. John's Church and we are chapel In any case, they are having a church parade next Sunday and I have promised to go fishing with Fred Jackson.

School is breaking up for the summer holidays next week. I will be glad of some extra time to spend with my friends and go fishing, but I will miss Nancy. If I have nothing better to do, I might hang around her house in case she comes out.

August. No more school for a month. Hooray! It is my birthday today. I'm eleven. I got lots of cards and - big surprise – one from Nancy. But, guess what? I've got a full size bike. Dad bought it second-hand. He bought new tyres and a saddle, fixed the brakes and painted it with black enamel. With the handlebars and saddle at their lowest, I can just reach the pedals. I am used to a two-wheeler so I can balance alright, but it took me a while to do a running start. I shall be able to go fishing in the river now with my cousins. It is eight miles to the best spots. It was too far on my little bike but I can do eight miles each way easily now.

I walked past Nancy's yesterday. She saw me through the window and came out. She was glad to see me. I thanked her for the card. Her Mam asked me in and gave me a cup of tea and a slice of cake. I enjoyed it.

Went fishing in the river with my older cousins, Colin and Les. Fishing in moving water isn't as easy as in a pond. The current takes your float away really fast and you have to pay line out quickly, otherwise it goes tight and the bait comes up to the top, I couldn't get the hang of it, so I fished near the edge where the current was slow. I caught two little roach. There was a head wind on the way back so cycling was hard, especially uphill. All the same I will be glad to have another go on the river next week – I think I know where I was going wrong.

September. Back to school. I am now in the top class of the Juniors. Our teacher is a man, Mr. Leech. He is very strict and canes us for the least thing. Nancy is in the same class, but we no longer sit together. The boys are on one side of the classroom and the girls on the other, but I can still see Nancy from where I sit. I walked home with her yesterday tea-time, but instead of turning off at the crossroads, I went as far as her street with her and then walked back.

There is the usual batch of tearful new starters in the Infants. They seem to get younger each year. Some of them aren't properly weaned, At playtime there are always a few mams outside the gates, giving their kids their breasts through the railings. The infants playground is next to ours and we can see what goes on. I'll bet the mams think we don't know what they are doing. It will all stop when the weather gets colder. In any case there is free milk every morning but I don't suppose it is the same. I can't remember.

I took a pair of Dad's shoes to Mr. Thompson to be mended. He works in a wooden hut in his garden. He gets cross if he is called a cobbler. He says he is a shoe repairer, not a cobbler. Dad says he learned shoe repairing at a rehabilitation centre after an accident in the pit. He has some dead sharp knives. That reminds me, I found the sheath knife that I bought at Cleethorpes under some clothes in one of Mam's drawers. I wonder how it got there? I will sneak it out when I have thought of somewhere to hide it.

The football season has started but I am not keen. I try to find an excuse when it's football at school, especially in bad weather. Dad isn't very interested in football either, but he does the pools. You can win a lot of money for a few pence if you pick the right teams. I post his coupon for him every week.

October. It's getting frosty in the mornings. Dad is keeping his greenhouse boiler stoked up. His chrysanthemums are coming into bloom ready for next month's show at the club. Went with Jeff Godwin to get some conkers. We know where all the best trees are. If you don't go too early you can pick them off the ground without having to knock them down. I soak mine in vinegar and then bake them a bit in the oven. It makes them dead hard. I had a sixteener last year but I am not doing so well this season.

Dad took me up to the top road to cheer the Jarrow marchers on. They are marching down to London to protest to the government about unemployment on the River Tyne. The Jarrow shipyard closed down and put nearly every man in the town on the dole. They get enough money to keep from starving but not enough for anything else. Dad took some fags to hand out as they passed. Some were playing mouth organs and some were whistling. We are lucky that our pit can sell its coal and keep its miners working.

Mr. Leech has spoken to the headmaster and they are putting me in for the grammar school scholarship. I will have to do a lot more reading and sums at home but Mr. Leech says that if I get to the grammar school, I will get a much better job or maybe even go to university. I don't know about that. I was looking forward to leaving school at fourteen and earning some money. But I don't want to go down the pit. I quite like the idea of going to a clean job in a smart suit. Anyway I will do my best and see what happens. Nancy would like to be a secretary or a typist.

November. Bad news! Nancy is leaving. Her Dad has finished at the pit. He is going down to Birmingham to work in a factory. He says that jobs are easier to get, the work is cleaner, the pay is better and they are building houses which ordinary people can buy for £1 a week through what is called a building society. I shall miss Nancy.

Bonfire night was great. Me and Jeff Godwin had been collecting old wood for weeks. I emptied my money box to spend on fireworks and Mam helped us to make a Guy Fawkes out of old clothes, stuffed with straw. Grandma made some treacle toffee. It was all over too soon. Bangers were still going off around the village when I went to bed. This morning there was a thick fog everywhere. You could hardly see your hand in front of you. I had to feel my way to school with my hand along the railings. Some kids didn't get there. You could taste the fumes from the pit heap on your lips.

Jim Kelly has been taken away. He has got TB – what some people call consumption. He has gone to somewhere called a sanatorium, where he will get good food and lots of fresh air. He might be away a year. He is the same age as me. His mam was in tears as they put him in the ambulance. I hope he gets better.

Went to the pictures to see *Captain Blood*. What a great film: pirates and sword fights and sea battles. Errol Flynn is real good at fencing.

December. Three boys have been hit by a car while they were crossing the road outside the school. They are all in hospital. One of them is very poorly; I hope he gets better. The driver will be for it; they were at a Belisha Beacon and he should have stopped. King Edward has given up his job; abdication I think they are calling it. He wants to marry a woman called Mrs. Simpson, but Mr. Baldwin, the Prime Minister, said he couldn't while he was king. His brother is now King George, the same as his dad only the sixth instead of the fifth. That makes three kings in one year. Mr. Leech says we will probably get another mug when King George is crowned next year. Anyhow, all the fuss has given us a new carol to sing this Christmas:

'Hark the Herald Angels sing,
Mrs. Simpson's pinched our King.'

I've made a list of what I would like for Christmas. It's not a long list with getting a bike for my birthday, but I could do with a new fishing rod. My old one is too short for river fishing – that's why I couldn't manage it properly. Anyway, I won't be going until the new season starts next June. It's too cold and there is too much water in the river.

Me and Jeff Godwin have started carol singing round the houses. We havn't made much money so far. Everybody makes excuses like 'it's too early' or 'somebody has already been'. I helped Mam to decorate the tree and put the trimmings up. The tree is an artificial one that we have had as long as I can remember. Mam won't have a real one because the needles drop and get everywhere. There are carols on the wireless nearly all the time now.

Got a smashing fishing rod for Christmas. Just what I wanted. I can't wait to try it out. Grandma and Grandad came round for Christmas Day. We had a chicken for dinner. Best of all I got a Christmas card from Nancy. I sent her one back.

I wonder what 1937 will be like and what I will be doing in a year's time. I don't even know which school I will be at. I don't know whether I am clever enough for the grammar school and I panic when I think about the scholarship exam. I get a lump in my throat when I think about Nancy.

A Very Personal Service

Connie Bull was not the most active prostitute in the village, but she was widely and affectionately known for her special services. She was a motherly sort of woman, around forty years of age, with long black hair, huge breasts and an expression that said 'go on, surprise me if you can'.

One of Connie's regular clients was Donald Cook, manager of the local branch of the Co-op. Donald was a middle-aged bachelor, balding, with a slight stoop and a habit of rubbing his hands together, especially when confronted personally by a customer. He tried to play the part of a strict, authoritarian boss, but his benevolent appearance and his gentle disposition defeated his attempts and his staff took advantage of his good nature. Donald, almost to his surprise, had risen through the store's hierarchy due to the Co-op's policy of internal promotion, accelerated considerably by the manpower demands of the Great War. Donald was an only child, whose father had been killed in a mining accident, when Donald was only a baby. He had been raised under careful maternal control and, outside of school, had had little contact with 'rough boys' or 'common girls', in consequence of which he was a loner and something of a social misfit. He had respected his mother and had dutifully looked after her during her long terminal illness.

Donald had met Connie when she had gone over the heads of his staff with a complaint about her weekly groceries delivery. With her wide experience of men and her sharply attuned instincts, she had quickly identified Donald as a potential client and had invited him to her flat, above the Excelsior Garage, for a chat. It had taken several chats to form an idea of Donald's needs and a process of trial and error had done the rest.

Donald fell into the habit of visiting Connie each Wednesday afternoon which was the store's half-day. They would have a chat over a cup of tea and Connie would use all her skills to make him feel comfortable and in sympathetic hands. Then she would deftly undress him, bathe him, dry

41

him, powder him, put a white nappy on him and put him to her breast. When he showed signs of becoming drowsy, Connie would help him into bed, tuck him in and quietly tiptoe out of the room, knowing that when she next looked in on him, Donald would need his nappy changing.

Ghosts

Charlie Bradshaw left school in 1932 at the age of fourteen. He was small for his age and did not really have the physique for mine work, but, in the early 'thirties, there were precious few alternatives in South Yorkshire, so Charlie applied for work at the pit. Like most new boys, he was put to work on the screens, picking out the dirt and stones, as the coal was graded into different sizes. Paradoxically, work on the screens, considered suitable for those who did not have the health or strength to work underground, was the dirtiest job in the pit. The vibrating mesh pans threw clouds of dust into the air, which the boys and elderly men, bending over the pans to pick out the refuse, could not avoid. Nor could they avoid the deafening noise that the reciprocating machinery continuously gave out.

Apart from short intervals, when he was put onto other work, Charlie persevered with the awful screen job until he was sixteen, at which age he would normally have gone onto heavy work underground. The under-manager realised that Charlie was just not cut out to be a miner, but he knew that he was a conscientious worker and he was reluctant to finish him. Fortunately, a job came up which the under-manager thought might just suit Charlie. The job was that of handyman to the mine surveyor. The surveyor was an important man in the pit, whose function was to plot the progress of each face and roadway on his drawings, to set out the headings for new and extended roadways and to keep check on roof and floor movements throughout the mine because, in a pit, nothing was stationary for long. The surveyor's handyman carried his equipment, kept it clean and serviceable, ran his errands and provided an additional pair of eyes and ears in the interests of safety underground. Charlie enjoyed his new job. The surveyor always explained what he was doing and why, because he believed that was the best way to keep a subordinate's interest and loyalty and to get the best out of him. He also treated Charlie with kindness and consideration, which was rare in mine work. Charlie, for his part, learned to respect his boss for his skill and knowledge and his friendly ways.

Inevitably, there came a day when Charlie's boss had to take measurements in a district which had not been worked since a terrible disaster, thirty years previously, when twenty-five men had been killed in an explosion. No sooner had they arrived in the old workings than then surveyor remembered that he had to make an important telephone call. He told Charlie he would not be long, warned him not to disturb anything and set off for the pit bottom, from where he could make his call. Standing there alone in almost total darkness was an eerie experience for Charlie and he could not stop thinking about all those miners who had walked into these workings, all those years ago, never to walk out again. Still legible, in the light from his safety lamp, were names, chalked on pillars, where bodies had been found, together with dates and the initials of those who had found them. Partly-filled coal tubs were still standing where they had been abandoned. Most poignant of all, here and there, an old water bottle or snap tin could be seen protruding from the stone and slack of the packing in the waste.

As he stood thinking about those poor lost souls, Charlie was horrified to hear a low moaning noise from somewhere in the darkness, further along the face. He stood rooted to the spot, petrified, imagining that the ghosts of the victims were still lying in agony, where they had fallen. He did not know how long he had been standing there, when another moan, louder this time, reverberated through the workings. Frightened out of his wits, Charlie dropped his equipment, took to his heels and ran all the way back to the pit bottom, without stopping for breath.

Charlie found out later that sheet metal brattices, used to direct the flow of ventilating air around the mine, could, if not properly supported, vibrate in the strong air current, giving out peculiar noises. This explanation went some way towards calming his fears, but Charlie knew, in his heart, that he could never again go, unaccompanied, into those ghostly old workings.

A Baby's Arm

The colliery company installed pit-head baths in 1934. The new building was divided into three sections: the dirty locker room, the shower room and the clean locker room. At the end of a shift, the men were to leave their working clothes in their dirty lockers, pass through the showers, dry themselves and dress in their street clothes in the clean locker room. A few of the older men resented the lack of privacy attending this arrangement and persisted in going home 'in their muck'. But the great majority of the miners considered the baths to be an enormous benefit. The virtual disappearance. from the streets of black-faced men in grimy clothes, transformed the image of coal mining. The young, single men, in particular, welcomed the freedom to travel to and from work, clean and decently dressed, and were no longer embarrassed by the prospect of being seen by young women in the state in which they emerged from the pit.

But to Alan Hill, the baths were a mixed blessing. Alan was a slim, handsome young chap whom nature had generously endowed in the genital area. His fame spread from the very first time that he emerged from the showers with his extraordinary appendage swinging between his thighs. One Friday, at the end of the morning shift, as Alan stood towelling himself in the locker room, one of his mates remarked that it was a fine day outside. 'I hope it keeps up for the weekend,' replied Alan. His reply was made in all innocence, but, from that moment, Alan could not pass another miner in the street without some crack about it keeping up for the weekend.

But Alan really became a legend on the day that the Overman walked through the locker room and caught sight of him naked. 'What on earth is that?' the deputy exclaimed, 'its like a b . . . . babies arm!' This outburst was overheard by most of Alan's shift mates and by the next day, the story of the baby's arm was being repeated throughout the pit.

Alan had recently married a girl from the town and, as yet, they had no family, so his wife, Sheila, was puzzled when she started receiving solicitous enquiries about the condition of the baby's arm. At first, she politely explained that she did not have a baby and that there must be some misunderstanding. But the knowing smiles which her explanation evoked soon made her realise that there must be something behind the questioning. She asked her husband several times if he knew what it was all about, but he seemed evasive on the subject. Eventually, after being embarrassed by remarks from a group of sniggering girls, she cornered Alan and demanded an explanation. Realising that she was now distressed, Alan sat down with her and, choosing his words carefully, related to her what had been the consequences, for him, of the opening of the new baths. Sheila was horrified. Alan was a loving husband and she was aware that she was not exactly deprived when it came to lovemaking, but she had not been promiscuous before meeting him, so she had no idea how exceptional he was.

The idea that most of the miners and their families now knew about Alan's distinctive anatomy and were probably conjecturing about their sex life was more than Sheila could stand. She packed her bags and returned home to her parents after telling Alan that she would rejoin him as soon as he had transferred to a pit in another village. Within three months, they had resettled on a pleasant council housing estate within walking distance of Alan's new pit. When Sheila, in the fullness of time, started a family, she was as thrilled and happy as any mother could be. But she never forgot what she had had to endure on account of those blasted pit-head baths.

A Pony Called Jack

Fred Griffith was a big, bad tempered Welshman. With his brother, Emlyn, he had left the Rhonda and its tragic scale of unemployment, in the early 1930s, and had moved to South Yorkshire. Here, miners who were sufficiently mobile could still find work in some of the more productive pits, which were able to turn out coal cheaply enough to sell in the depressed market.

The two brothers had found lodgings with a middle aged couple whose two sons were also miners, but whilst Emlyn had settled in comfortably with the family, Fred's unpleasant disposition had worn thin his welcome and he had been asked to go. He had subsequently moved from one squalid lodging house to another, his temper worsening with each move.

Although Fred was a 'big hitter' as the higher-earning hewers were called, his offensiveness to his workmates disrupted the harmony of the coal face and, after several warnings, the overman removed him and put him on haulage. The consequent drop in earnings and loss of prestige only served to make Fred more angry and he was even less pleased when he was taken off rope haulage and sent to another district as a pony driver. He was given a pony called Jack and, as his mean reputation had preceded him, he was warned to treat Jack kindly.

Jack was one of the best ponies in the pit. He was docile, reliable and hard working. His only fault was that, occasionally, when being coupled to tubs, he would shuffle backwards slightly, thereby relieving the load on himself for an instant, and if he was facing up an incline, each of the tubs behind him would roll back an inch or two to take up the slack. This could be quite dangerous for the driver, if he happened to be coupling an additional tub when Jack did his shuffle. Fred was not warned about this and since he took little interest in Jack as a living creature, he had not studied the pony's habits. Inevitably, there came a day when, as Fred was coupling a fourth tub, Jack eased the strain and the fingers of Fred's right hand were crushed in the coupling.

Instead of going straight to the first aid station at the pit bottom, Fred, blinded by rage, chocked the wheels, uncoupled Jack from the first tub, walked him back along the track and coupled him to the last, facing down the incline. He then beat Jack with a shovel to make the poor animal move as quickly as he could. After a few yards, the momentum of the four tubs on the incline took over, forcing Jack to gallop faster and faster until he fell and the tubs piled up on top of him. He died instantly.

It was obvious to the officials what had happened and Fred was immediately sent out of the pit. He was sacked for cruelty to the pony and prosecuted by the Mines Inspectorate for breeches of the safety regulations. No other pit in the area would employ him and, within a few weeks, he found himself heading back to South Wales and the dole queue.

Sweat

In 1934, the Town Council elected a woman mayor. Although she was a Labour councillor, the new mayor was unmistakeably middle class: very authoritarian, very dignified and always impeccably turned out. In planning her year of office, the new civic leader decided that she would like, as one of her first official engagements, to visit one of the large coal mines, with which the town was ringed, and which had brought work and prosperity to the area.

The staff of the chosen pit spent weeks preparing for the visit, cleaning and tidying, both above and below ground, and painting everything that would stand still long enough. On the morning of the visit, daylight broke to reveal a crudely-painted cartoon on the newly whitewashed gable-end of the blacksmith's shop, immediately facing the colliery entrance. It depicted a pit pony, with a chain of office around its neck, and under it the caption: 'Welcome to our mare'. When the manager saw it, as he arrived for work, he forgot the polite language in which he was rehearsing his speech of welcome to the mayor and described, as only a pitman could, what he would do to the culprit, if he caught him. But the offender was never identified. His artwork was whitewashed over just in time for the Mayor's arrival.

After showing the mayoral party around the surface workings, the manager invited them into the cage and signalled for the descent. After overcoming her initial alarm at the speed with which they were hurtling down, her worship demanded to know why they were going back up. The manager explained that this was the misleading sensation that most people experienced when going down in the cage for the first time and that, in reality, their descent had not been interrupted.

As the party reached the pit bottom and entered the main roadway, the manager explained the layout of the pit, the haulage arrangements and the pillar and stall method of extracting coal. He also pointed out that, for geophysical reasons, it was very hot in the workings they would be visiting. After about a quarter of a mile, the manager led the way into a low tunnel and the party emerged into a working stall. To their left was an area from which the coal had already been extracted, with pillars of coal at intervals, left to support the roof, whilst to their right was the working coal face. Peering through the gloom, the mayor could see two men, one of whom was shovelling coal into a tub, whilst the other, completely naked except for his helmet, knee pads and clogs, was lying on his side, swinging a pick at the coal face. 'That man has nothing on,' gasped the mayor. 'Where are your clothes, young man?'

'That's them hanging on that nail,' replied the miner.

'Well, put them on at once,' ordered the Mayor.

'I can't, they're wet through' said the lad. Whereupon her worship took the singlet and shorts off the nail, wrung them out, handed them to the embarrassed miner and hurried out of the stall.

As the party returned to the pit bottom, the mayor's indignation turned to curiosity. 'Where did that young man get the water to wash his clothes?' she asked.

'That wasn't water' replied the manager, 'That was sweat.'

Throughout the remainder of the visit, the manager could not help noticing the mayor surreptitiously scrubbing her hands on her handkerchief, over and over again.

As Others See Us

Dr. Robert Erskine moved from Edinburgh to South Yorkshire in 1910 when he was in his mid-thirties. He had been a junior partner in an Edinburgh practice, but he had grown tired of doing most of the work for a small share of the profits and when he heard that the rapidly expanding new coalfield was crying out for doctors, he decided on a change of environment. A pit village surgery was far removed from the fashionable practice that Erskine had pictured for himself as a medical student, but at least he was working for himself. His earnings now bore a reasonable relationship to his efforts and when he was appointed medical officer to the colliery company, he acquired a second, although hard-earned, source of income.

Dr. Erskine was a big man with a firm but kindly way of dealing with his patients and he soon earned the respect of the community. He married the daughter of a business family in the town, who bore him two sons, one of whom followed his father's footsteps as a general practitioner, whilst the other went into his grandfather's business. Erskine sat on the Board of the village's cottage hospital and did whatever surgery was within his capacity. This kept him in good practice for whatever he might be faced with down the pit. He also kept abreast of progress in medicine by subscribing to the most authoritative medical journals. Erskine was lucky in that he had few major emergencies to deal with. There were the usual epidemics of measles, chicken pox, whooping cough and mumps; there was the occasional case of meningitis, sometimes fatal, and tuberculosis was still carrying off teenagers and young adults. But hardly a week went by without a call to the colliery to deal with torn flesh and broken bones, usually under the most difficult physical conditions.

The Great War came and went with, thankfully, less impact on the village than many other parts of the nation. There was a surge of enlistment by young men in 1914 and those who went bore their share of the appalling casualties, but the government soon realised that the war effort needed coal miners almost as badly as it needed soldiers and the recruiting sergeants began to turn them away.

But Erskine was never short of a challenge and the years seemed to roll by ever more quickly. As he approached his mid-sixties he began to feel that he had had enough. The constant succession of crowded surgeries, long rounds of home visits, disturbed nights and underground emergencies had taken their toll and he was beginning to feel his age. As the war clouds gathered once again over Europe, Erskine decided, at the age of sixty-five, that it was time for him to hand over to a younger man. At the news of his impending retirement, the colliery managers and the village elders came together to give him a farewell dinner. Now Erskine knew all about retirement dinners; he seemed to have attended more and more of other people's in recent years and he knew that there would be well-meaning comments about his years of service to the community. He decided that in response he would say something about his feelings for the village and its inhabitants. He guessed that a reporter from the local weekly would be there, so he realised that he would have to think carefully about what he was going to say.

The event went well. After a few drinks and an enjoyable meal at the only hotel that the village boasted, the pit manager rose to reflect on Erskine's important role in the community, to wish him a long and happy retirement and to present him with a memento in the form of a miner, sculpted out of a block of coal, complete with pick and shovel, helmet and lamp. Erskine responded suitably to the good wishes, acknowledged the thoughtful gift and went on to say:

'Thank you for welcoming me into your community all those years ago and for your unfailing friendship and support during those years. I have never, for an instant, regretted my decision to settle in your midst. Coming, as I did, from a Scottish city to a South Yorkshire village was a bit of a culture shock, but my work and my association with you rapidly proved a pleasure and a privilege. I have always seen so much to respect and admire here: the pride which the miners take in their arduous and dangerous work; the dignity with which they walk to and from the pit; the familiarity and comradeship which they show for one another, borne of facing danger together underground and the care and attention which they lavish on their allotments and their pigeons. The miner's wives too have my admiration for the cleanliness and neatness of their homes; the pride and care that they take in their children; their never-ending battle against dust and grime and their prudence and skill in managing their housekeeping money'.

'I applaud the efforts of the teachers to give the children a good start in life, not always under the most favourable conditions, and I salute the nurses and midwives, who have never failed to support me in my work and who can be seen, at all hours of the day and night, bringing comfort and relief to those in their charge. I also esteem the work of our local authority and its employees who provide our essential services and maintain public order. And I must express my admiration of those talented people who, through music, drama or sporting prowess bring excitement and entertainment to us lesser mortals, to brighten our leisure hours and enrich our lives'.

'But there are features of life in the village that I do not admire. I detest excessive drinking, the results of which I have frequently had to deal with. Drunkenness is a blot on society and a blight on family life, health and happiness; it results in violence, sickness and poverty. Equally, I loathe all forms of gambling and their abominable consequences. Gambling feeds on greed, envy and weakness of character; quickly or slowly, it destroys those who fall prey to it; it takes comfort, warmth and happiness out of the home and food out of the family's mouths. I have never known of a gambler who has won, in the long run, but I have known of quite a few who have reduced themselves and their families to poverty and misery'.

'At the risk of straying into the world of politics, I believe that the best health, welfare and education services should be available to everyone, regardless of status, occupation or income. In my opinion, public ownership of the coal mines and other essential industries would benefit their employees, their customers and the national economy and remove much injustice. In particular, it is my view that if wages were determined by the demands of the job and its value to society, the coal miner would be as well paid as the doctor or the lawyer'.

The Doctor concluded with some heartfelt remarks about the kindness and fellowship that the community had shown him over the years, his good wishes for the future and his confidence that the village and its inhabitants would be equal to the approaching conflict which now appeared inevitable.

Three days later, the local weekly newspaper dropped onto Erskine's doormat. As he scanned the report of his farewell dinner, Erskine shook his head. It was accurate and fair as far as it went, but every word about social problems, state ownership of industry, health and welfare provisions and miner's wages had been edited out. It would take six years of war and a wake-up call from those who fought it, to make the establishment receptive to ideas of that sort.

THE SECOND WORLD WAR

Absentee

Ken Smith was a filler on No. 5 face, but he was also a versatile musician. Coal miners were traditionally keen on music; perhaps there was something about the brutality of their work that drew them to it. Not that Ken looked much like a musician; he was in his early thirties, but he looked older, with a paunch, heavy features and a receding hairline. Ken lived with his widowed mother, who doted on him. His father had died of silicosis after forty years in the mines. Being waited on hand and foot by his mother suited Ken and although he had plenty of women acquaintances, he had never had any inclination to leave home. Ken played the cornet in the colliery band, but he could play most brass instruments and was especially fond of the saxophone. Throughout the war, on most evenings except Sundays, there was a dance on, either at one of the town's ballrooms, or in the welfare hall of one of the surrounding mining villages. Ken moonlighted, as his shifts permitted, with one or other of the local dance bands and because he could fill in on several different instruments, he was always in demand.

But going to bed late on several consecutive nights was not conducive to getting up in time for work, especially when Ken was on the morning shift and had to be at the pit bottom by six am. His mother would call him repeatedly and do all she could to get him out of bed, but often to no avail. As a result, Ken was often 'gated' and sometimes he would sleep in and make no attempt to get to work that day. The trouble was that, under the wartime emergency regulations, absence from a coal mine 'without due cause' was a criminal offence and Ken was committing it. He was warned several times by the under-manager who, under the regulations, had to report his repeated absences to the local office of the Ministry of Labour and National Service. But Ken enjoyed his dance band engagements and they were his priority. In any case, they paid more than his pit job, so the possibility of being sacked didn't worry him.

But the wheels were turning in the Regional office of the Ministry and there came a morning when Mrs. Smith answered a knock on the door to find a policeman holding out a buff envelope. It contained a summons to her son, to present himself to the town's magistrate's court, to answer a charge of unlawfully absenting himself from his work as a coal miner.

Ken was not unduly worried. What was a fine of a few pounds compared to the money he was earning from his two jobs. He engaged a solicitor to speak for him and attended court on the due date. He could not plead other than 'guilty' but his solicitor said, in mitigation, that Ken was helping the war effort, not only in mining badly-needed coal, but in helping to keep up the spirits of other workers and members of the armed forces, by playing for them at dances, whenever his work allowed. The lawyer added:

'If this young man is sent to prison, it will not only be a blot on his hitherto blameless character, but will deprive the public of his contribution to the maintenance of morale during these dark days.'

In telling of it afterwards, Ken said bitterly: 'Until my own solicitor mentioned it, nobody had said anything about going to prison, but as soon as the magistrates got their heads together, I got three months hard labour.'

Ken did not enjoy his incarceration: the discipline was oppressive, the warders brutal and the food atrocious. When he was released, he moved to another pit to avoid the inevitable leg-pulling by his former workmates. He resumed his dance band engagements, but not on a scale that would affect his mine work. The thought of the sentence that a second conviction would bring made his mother determined that he would never again lose a shift through sleeping-in. When the war ended and the labour regulations were lifted, Ken raised two fingers to the pits, moved to the Midlands and formed his own successful dance band.

My Yank

By the time Hilda Dakin was thirty, she had given birth to seven children and looked twice her age. Her husband, George, was good at his job at the coal face, but he was a waster in all other respects. He gave Hilda no help with the house or family, spent most of his free time between the pub and the club and kept back half his pay to fund his drinking, smoking and gambling. Debilitated by a poor diet and frequent child-bearing, it was all Hilda could do to keep the children clothed and put food on the table; she had no energy left to do anything about her appearance or to do justice to the housework. The house was untidy, dirty and smelly. The garden consisted of a bare patch of earth, where the younger children played, surrounded by a jungle of weeds. The family lived in squalor.

In 1936, after the last child was born, George committed the ultimate betrayal and left home. He went without warning or explanation and left no clue as to his intentions; he thought only of himself as he always had. There was a rumour that George had gone to work in the Staffordshire pits, but his wife and family never heard from him again. Hilda was forced onto 'relief' and although she hadn't believed it possible, she was even worse off than before. When the war came in 1939, she had all the worry of rationing, the blackout, gas masks and air raids to cope with, as well as the scarcity of almost everything necessary for running a house and family. The only glimmer of relief was that the older children were getting big enough to help around the house, whilst the eldest, Betty, had turned fourteen and started work in 1938, since when she had been contributing most of her small wage to the family's meagre income.

Betty had been forced to grow up fast. She started looking after her younger siblings when she was little more than a toddler herself. Her mother's reliance on her meant that she had little opportunity to go out and play with other children. For the same reason, she frequently had to miss school whenever there was any sort of domestic crisis. But the unfair demands on her made Betty more resourceful than other girls her age. She was also early in her physical development. When Betty left school, she was already beginning to look like a woman and by the time she reached sixteen, although she could not be described as pretty, she had a figure that turned heads and attracted wolf whistles everywhere she went.

Betty's job was at a clothing factory in the town. Before the war, the place had a reputation as a 'sweat shop', but it had now acquired the respectability of being engaged on essential war work, making uniforms and special equipment for the armed forces. Betty's work as a machinist was arduous and monotonous, but she enjoyed the chatter with the other girls and 'music while you work' which was broadcast continually over loudspeakers in the workshops. Betty and Jean, the girl at the next machine, exchanged confidences and became firm friends. The differences in their past lives made Betty realise how little she knew beyond her own family and neighbourhood and how little friendship and affection she had experienced. At Jean's suggestion, they started to go out together: to the cinema, to dances and to anywhere where they might get into conversation with boys. Jean was prettier and more socially adept than Betty and had lots of young men wanting to date her. Betty, with her stunning figure, but little conversation, seemed always to attract the wrong sort, the sort with only one thing on their minds.

In 1943, an American army base was set up on the far side of the town from the village and the bus services in that direction were soon overloaded with young women wanting to find out what the Yanks were like. Jean persuaded Betty to take a ride out to the camp one Sunday afternoon and together with other girls, they began to stroll around the perimeter fence. They were assailed with all sorts of comments and propositions from within the compound which, although flattering and spoken in the fascinating accent that they had only heard at the pictures, they studiously ignored. But when they had almost completed their circuit of the camp and were approaching the main gate again, two much more circumspect young soldiers said 'Hello' and asked their names. The boys were polite and, unlike most of their comrades, were not brash or pushy. Their names were Joe and Danny. They told the girls which parts of the United States they had come from, what their lives had been like before being drafted and what their jobs were in the army. By the time they left, the girls had agreed to see the two soldiers again the following week.

Before a month had passed, Betty was seeing Joe at every opportunity. Joe was a motor mechanic, which often afforded him the use of a jeep, thereby enabling him to meet Betty near her home in the village. When Joe only had an hour or two free, Betty would take a bus to the camp and they would go for a walk in the nearby woods. Betty never took Joe home because the family still lived in squalid conditions, which she would have been ashamed for him to see. But, to friends and neighbours, she made no secret of the fact that she was going out with an American. If anybody asked her where she was going, she would reply, without hesitation, 'To see my Yank'. Her nylon stockings, 'Luck Strike' cigarettes and the large chocolate bars which she passed on to her brothers and sisters, were evidence, to the whole neighbourhood, that she was friendly with a generous GI. Betty became familiar with the cocktail lounges of the town's hotels, sat in the best seats at the cinema and took great pleasure in being seen riding at Joe's side in his jeep. On several evenings a week, the parked jeep told neighbours where Betty and Joe were saying their long 'good-nights'. In 1939, when war was finally accepted as inevitable, an emergency hospital had been built in the village. It was intended for wounded servicemen and civilian bomb victims; it also had spare wards and operating theatres in case the town's main hospital should be bombed and needed to be evacuated. The building was surrounded by a thick, high wall of sandbags as a protection against bomb blast and the access to each door took the form of a narrow passage between the sandbags which, in the blackout, became an impenetrably dark canyon. It was in one of these canyons that the couple, on most evenings, had their last moments of passion before parting. Neighbours, passing and noting the empty jeep, got into the habit of shouting 'goodnight Betty' into the passage; they sometimes received a muffled reply and sometimes not, according to what Betty was doing at the time.

In the early spring of 1944, neighbours could not help noticing that Betty was putting on weight and it was all in one place. She made no attempt to disguise the fact that she was pregnant and was perfectly happy, believing that Joe and the United States Army would look after her. But Joe was now preparing for a very different event, which took up more and more of his time. It was late May and 'D Day', the day for the Allied attack on Hitler's Europe, was fast approaching. On the last day of the month, one of Betty's friends saw her, heavily pregnant, standing at the bus stop on the opposite side of the road. 'Where are you off to Betty?' she shouted.

'I'm going to see my Yank,' replied Betty as usual. But Betty's bus journey was not the joyful event that it had always been in the past. She knew that something had come between Joe and her and she had a presentiment that, today, she would find out what. When she alighted from the bus her fears were confirmed; she could see no activity in or around the camp, except for two armed military policemen on duty at the gate. 'What's happened?' asked Betty in dismay.

'This camp is closed,' replied one of the MPs 'and everyone has left.'

'Can you tell me where they have gone?' asked Betty, her voice quivering.

'I can't give anyone any information at all,' said the MP curtly.

Betty retraced her steps to the bus stop in tears. She hadn't seen her Yank after all and she knew in her heart that she was unlikely ever to see him ever again.

Pin Money

On pay days, a miner would present his numbered lamp check at the window of the wages office and receive his earnings, in cash, in a small copper cylinder bearing the same number as his check. Most miners tipped up all their pay to their wives and took back a mutually agreed amount for their pocket money. But the more selfish of them did not tell their wives exactly how much they earned and regularly with-held part of their pay to supplement the pocket money that had been agreed. The undeclared amount was usually referred to as 'pin money.' Pin money was regarded by some as legitimate retaliation against demanding wives, but, in practice, it meant extra indulgence in beer, cigarettes and gambling at the expense of the family's standard of living.

But wives too had their version of pin money. Most houses had gas lighting, which was paid for through penny-in-the-slot meters. The sealed coin boxes were emptied monthly by the gas company collector who checked the cash against the meter reading. The coin mechanism was not precise and the gas company preferred to have any error in their favour and pay back the excess at each reading. For this reason, housewives looked forward to the monthly visits of the gas man in the expectation that they would get some cash back in their hands. This windfall was, by common consent, never declared to husbands, who were usually working or asleep when the gas man called, but was kept aside for an occasional treat.

Jack Lambert was an inveterate pin money cheat, but he was neither a heavy drinker nor smoker and he did not gamble, so his hoard of cash built up. It brought with it the problem of where to hide it. He tried several places around the house, but had to abandon each one in turn when he thought that discovery by his wife was imminent. He finally hit on the idea of a secret compartment in the cupboard of his allotment hut. Using his skill as an amateur joiner, Jack enclosed a small space behind a drawer, secured by a secret panel, which only he knew how to release. It was just big enough to hold an old tobacco tin, in which he kept the money in tightly folded pound and ten shilling notes.

One bitterly cold evening in the January of 1941, the air raid sirens went as Jack was walking to the pit for the night shift. 'I reckon Sheffield will be getting it again tonight,' he thought to himself.

Safe underground, Jack thought no more about air raids, or the war, as he got on with his work. But as he and his mates emerged into the still dark streets on the following morning, they were greeted with the news that there had been an incendiary raid on the village. Fortunately, they were told, the fire bombs had landed on the allotments and the fields beyond and nobody had been hurt. But Jack began to worry. Instead of going directly home, he went straight to the allotments where, in the dim light of the early dawn, a pitiful sight met his gaze. A whole row of huts, pigeon crees and greenhouses had been destroyed along the line where the stick of incendiaries had fallen. The fire brigade had done what they could, but the ramshackle wooden buildings had been liberally coated with tar to keep out the weather and they had gone up like tinder. Among them was Jack's own hut, now a heap of charred timbers and ashes. Jack poked about among the rubble until he found his tobacco tin. With trembling fingers he opened the tin to find his worst fears realised. The growing daylight revealed the crumbling grey ashes of incinerated pound and ten shilling notes. After staring uncomprehendingly for a few moments, Jack upturned the tin and the ashes blew away on the early morning breeze.

Jack walked home with a heavy heart. There had been over a hundred pounds in that tin and, to a working man in the 1940s, a hundred pounds was a lot of money. He could not believe that it was all gone. His brain was working overtime, trying to think of ways of recovering his loss, but there were none. He could not do anything about it and, what's more, he could not even tell anybody about it. That was the trouble with pin money.

Nurse Ellen

Nurse Ellen Cooper was the district midwife. She was a big, handsome woman in her late thirties. She had beautiful red-brown hair which, in her teens, fell almost to her waist, but which, for the practical purposes of her job, she now kept trimmed to collar length. She had a full figure, a beaming smile and a sense of humour that came from years of trying to inject a little light-heartedness into tense situations. Ellen had no children of her own. Her husband, Tom, was a flight sergeant in the RAF; he was in charge of a bomber maintenance crew in North Africa, servicing the aircraft which were attacking Rommel's tanks and supply ships. Tom had joined the regular air force in 1930 to escape the dole queue and had married Ellen three years later. They had decided to postpone starting a family until Tom's service was up, which was to have been 1940, but would not now be until the war was over. Ellen now regretted that decision and desperately hoped that Tom would be home before she was too old to be a mum.

All Nurse Ellen's clients and potential clients knew of her little weakness: she was partial to a glass of sweet sherry. After most confinements, the patient or a member of the family would discreetly hand her a cheap bottle of her favourite tipple in appreciation of her services. Since there were few days on which Ellen did not attend at least one delivery, her stock never ran low. Not that she was ever the worse for it; she always remained in full command of her professional faculties and in firm charge of each delivery. On her journeys between patients, her bicycle was never seen to wobble. Ellen's work brought her into contact with both great happiness and extreme misery; perhaps there were times when the misery seemed to outweigh the happiness and she needed something to keep her spirits up.

On receiving notification of a pregnancy, Ellen would visit the mother-to-be on two or three occasions, prior to the confinement, to check on progress. On one of these preliminary visits, she was surprised to be told that the call had been made on behalf of the girl next door. The expectant mother was a single girl who had confided in the neighbour, but was afraid to tell her stern mother. Since the time of her confinement was drawing near and since, strangely enough, her mother had not noticed her condition, the neighbour had decided to take the initiative.

Ellen braced herself for the encounter. Her knock on the door was answered by the girl's mother.

'What do you want,' she demanded.

'I've come to see your daughter,' replied Ellen.

'What do you want with her?'

'I believe that she is pregnant.'

'How dare you?' exclaimed the indignant woman, 'my daughter has never had anything to do with men.'

Nurse Ellen went back to the front gate, shaded her eyes with her hand and looked up and down the street.

'What are you looking for?' asked the mother.

'I'm looking for men on camels,' quipped Ellen, 'the last time this happened, three wise men appeared from the East!'

. . .

Mrs Jackson was expecting twins; but Nurse Ellen had delivered her share of twins in her time, so she was not worried. The first baby appeared without any complications. The midwife freshened herself up at the kitchen sink and settled back for a yarn with the neighbouring women helpers while they waited for the second baby to arrive. It too presented no undue problems, so Ellen began to pack her equipment into the black bag attached to the handlebars of her bicycle, while the helpers cleaned up the mother and tidied the room. Just as Ellen was about to leave, one of the helpers nudged her arm and drew her attention to the patient who was showing signs of going into labour for the third time.

'Quick!' cried Ellen, 'close those b . . . . curtains, I think the light is attracting them.'

. . .

Mrs. Aldershaw had a difficult labour. Although it was her fifth, she was now well into her forties; her body was not as supple as it had been and she needed stitches.

The father came home from the morning shift at the pit to find the midwife at the front gate. 'What's happening?' he asked.

'Your wife has had a baby boy,' replied Ellen, 'but she needs stitching and I am waiting for the doctor.'

'Ask him to put an extra stitch in for me,' joked the father.

'If I ask him to do anything for you,' retorted Ellen, 'it will be to cut off that b . . . . thing of yours that has caused all this trouble!'

SAILOR BEWARE

During the mid-war years, Michael Rafferty was a familiar sight, sitting nonchalantly on the front gate of his parent's home, between shifts at the pit. He was in his early thirties, pleasant looking, with a shock of dark brown, curly hair that never seemed to need a comb. His mother and father had emigrated from Ireland around 1910, when they heard that there was work in the South Yorkshire mines and Michael had been born a few months later. At fourteen, he had followed his father down the pit and, like most mineworkers, he was exempt from call-up. Michael still lived with his parents and had inherited their soft, West of Ireland brogue, with which, it was said, he could charm the birds off the trees. He had had a succession of girl friends, but had never been tempted to leave home, where his mother waited on him, hand and foot.

Neighbours assumed that sitting on the gate was Michael's way of being sociable and getting some fresh air between sleep and work, but it was a bit more purposeful than that. Toward the far end of the street lived Eileen Watson and her two children: a boy of seven and a girl of five, both at primary school. Eileen was twenty-eight. Her husband, Fred, was a sailor who, because of the demands of wartime naval service, she rarely saw. Eileen had imprudently got into the habit of chatting with Michael, whenever she passed him in his customary posture, on her way to and from the shops. Starved of affection, she soon fell under the spell of his Celtic charm. One morning, as Eileen opened her front bedroom window, she saw Michael in his usual place on the gate and waved. He waved back and a few minutes later she heard a tapping on her back door. Michael had arrived covertly via the back lane which, being lined with the coal houses and privies of the two streets it served, was free of prying eyes and, except for washdays and coal delivery days, was usually deserted. Eileen was surprised and disturbed by Michael's audacity, but she was in no hurry to send him away. When he finally went, it was on the understanding that, if he saw her open her

69

bedroom window again, he would take it as an invitation to pay her another visit. From that day on, Michael spent even more time sitting on the gate and the benefit was not always limited to fresh air and gossip.

Michael and Eileen's relationship was interrupted occasionally by Fred's infrequent spells of leave from the navy, but resumed more intensely than before, after each separation. Inevitably, neighbours began to have suspicions. Total discretion is difficult to sustain in a small mining community. Michael's mother had known almost from the start, but seeing how happy her son was, she had turned a blind eye. But she now began to detect knowing looks from her neighbours and started to worry. When Eileen began showing unmistakeable signs of pregnancy, neighbouring women started relating her visible condition to the dates of her husband's leaves and were doubtful that the baby could be his, but nobody could be certain. When a lovely baby boy was born, suspicions were put aside and a great fuss was made of him as he lay in his pram at Eileen's front door.

There was a little crowd of women around the pram one afternoon when Peter's mother approached, unsteadily, on her way home from a liquid lunch with some of her cronies. Full of gin and good cheer, Mrs. Rafferty pushed her way through the onlookers and peered at the baby. 'Oh! The little darling,' she exclaimed, 'and sure isn't he the living image of our Peter?'

Mrs. Rafferty knew, from the sharp intake of breath around her, that she had said something she oughtn't, but, in her befuddled state, she was not sure what. She only knew that as she moved away, a lot of excited chatter burst out among the little crowd.

That evening, an unsigned letter dropped into the village post box, addressed to Able Seaman Frederick Watson. It caught up with Fred at his next port of call and, after a brief interview with his captain, he was granted compassionate leave. Neighbours could only surmise what took place between Fred and Eileen, but the truth must have come out, because Peter was not seen on the gate again for a very long time and, when he did finally reappear, he was not quite so good-looking, nor as charming as people remembered him.

The prospect of an encounter with Fred, every time he came home on leave, did not appeal to Peter, and he came to the reluctant conclusion that there was no longer a place for him in the village. He went to work at a pit in the Midlands and he never saw Eileen or his son again, although his mother kept him informed of the boy's progress. Fred was demobilised at the end of the war, took a job on the railway and proved an exemplary husband and father, drawing no distinction between Eileen's three children.

Look, Duck and Vanish

On the evening of 14 May 1940, as the British Expeditionary Force withdrew towards Dunkirk and a German invasion of Britain seemed inevitable, Anthony Eden, Secretary of State for War, made a radio broadcast announcing that a British home defence force was to be formed immediately and would be known as the Local Defence Volunteers, or LDV. From the early hours of the following day, men gathered in public halls, community halls and church halls, in all parts of the nation, where hundreds of thousands of them offered their services in defence of their homeland. The village was no exception. Since most of the volunteers were miners, it was natural that the new force should be closely associated with the pit. Those men who had served in the First World War found themselves being nominated as officers and NCOs. The hierarchy began to resemble that of the colliery with the under manager as commanding officer.

On the following Saturday the first parade was called. The volunteers had neither weapons nor uniforms, of course, and very little idea of what was expected of them. However, they began to drill and were asked to bring to the next parade a weapon of some sort: a shot gun or air gun if they had one or, failing all else, a broom handle or wooden stake. The numbers were large enough to correspond to a company in the regular army so they were divided into platoons, each with an officer, a sergeant and several corporals.

The first item of uniform with which the volunteers were issued was a khaki armband with the letters LDV in black. The acronym inevitably invited comic interpretations and the one that stuck was the cynical 'look, duck and vanish.' This did little for esprit de corps and, in August 1940, on the personal order of Prime Minister Churchill, the force was renamed the Home Guard. The arm band was quickly replaced by a khaki denim overall with 'Home Guard' shoulder flashes. Before the end of the year, most units had received the serge battledress, trousers and greatcoat of the regular army, distinguished by black leather belt and gaiters in place of the khaki webbing of the regulars. They were subsequently issued with boots, steel helmets and gas masks.

Rifles appeared within weeks of the force forming and many hours were spent removing the thick coating of grease in which they had been preserved since the First World War. Ammunition was limited to five rounds per man. Sten guns, too, soon found their way into Home Guard service; they were cheap and cheerful hand-held machine guns, which could be quickly turned out by almost any engineering workshop and were made in their hundreds of thousands, but not always to reliable standards. Pride of place went to the Bren gun, which was a very accurate, highly reliable light machine gun, with an integral tripod, which could be carried almost as easily as a rifle. Each platoon eventually acquired its own Bren gun and there was keen competition to be its guardian. Hand grenades were stocked at Company headquarters and their effectiveness was later increased by an attachment to a rifle, which enabled them to be fired with a special cartridge, giving them a much wider range than when hand-thrown.

A big improvement in organisation and training took place when Home Guard units became attached to regular army regiments, which began to provide instruction and supervision. The village company found itself attached to a famous Yorkshire infantry regiment. Gradually, an efficient fighting force began to emerge. But, as in most walks of life, it is not the achievement which lives on but the mistakes and the laughs.

...

Towards midnight on 8 September 1940, all members of the Home Guard throughout the nation were alerted and ordered to report to their headquarters with weapons and ammunition. Each company had a number of despatch riders, mainly on bicycles, one of whose jobs was to call out individual members in an emergency, which they now did. All units remained on alert throughout the night, at check points and look-out posts, expecting at any moment to face invading German troops. Nothing happened and at 08.00 hours on the following morning they were all stood down. What had lead to the alert was never disclosed, but the Home Guard had come of age and each member had had his courage and resolution tested. For years afterwards there circulated the apocryphal story of the company commander who, on that fateful night, as he sent his men out to defend Britain, had said to them: 'Now remember, men, you are facing a ruthless enemy, who has no mercy on those who oppose him, so make every bullet count and save the last one for yourself. Turning to his adjutant he asked 'How many rounds of ammunition do we have Lieutenant?'

'One each, Sir' came the reply!

. . .

On a Sunday morning in the late autumn of 1940, 'B' platoon were having Sten gun training on the army range, with a regular sergeant weapons instructor in charge and Lieutenant Baxter of the village Home Guard looking on. Harry Rainer, whose customary weapons were a shovel and pick at the coal face, was taking his turn at firing the Sten. Now because of the fine tolerances needed by the gun's repeater mechanism, some manufacturers had difficulty in meeting the specification and the Sten had a reputation for jamming; on this occasion, Harry's did. Forgetting all he had been taught about weapons safety, Harry turned around and with the gun pointing straight at the lieutenant and his finger still on the trigger, he complained:

'This b . . . . gun's not working.'

The horrified lieutenant froze to the spot, but the sergeant quickly picked up a rifle and, swinging it by the barrel, knocked the Sten out of Harry's hands. The gun fell harmlessly to the ground, while the air turned blue with a torrent of expletives that only a British Army NCO can muster. Harry was never trusted with a weapon again. As a punishment and a perpetual reminder of his lapse, he was confined to menial admin duties for the remainder of his Home Guard service.

. . .

One night in January 1941 the village was peppered with incendiaries and several buildings were set alight. One semi-detached house was burning fiercely and as the fire brigade prepared to tackle the blaze, they became aware of loud bangs from the adjoining house. In the hysteria of the times, they concluded that either German parachutists had landed or that the crew of a damaged enemy aircraft had bailed out and had occupied the house from which they were now firing. The firemen were not trained to deal with the enemy, so the Home Guard was called out. A platoon led by a lieutenant slowly advanced towards the house, prepared for any eventuality. Sporadic bangs like rifle fire could still be heard, but no-one was hit and no damage could be observed. Eventually the lieutenant, his heart thumping, kicked open the front door and, followed by his best men, entered and cautiously started checking each room in turn. The bangs were still occurring and, following the noise, they finally discovered its source. The absent occupier was apparently a home brewer and countless bottles of his best bitter were lined up in a spare bedroom. The heat from the burning house next door had raised the pressure in the tightly corked bottles, which were bursting, one by one, with a sound like gun-fire. There were red faces in the village the following morning and although the embarrassment gradually gave way to smiles, the assault on 54, The Grove would always be remembered as the village's most inglorious moment of the war.

...

In the spring of 1941, the village company of the Home Guard had an official photograph taken and every member received a copy. In June of that year, when Germany attacked the Soviet Union and the threat of an invasion of Britain greatly receded, it was jokingly rumoured that Hitler had seen a copy of the company photograph and had decided that he would rather face the Red Army.

...

In September 1944, as the remnants of the German army retreated towards their own borders, the Home Guard was disbanded. Standing-down parades and farewell dinners were held in towns and villages across the nation. All weapons and equipment were recalled and the members went their separate ways, never knowing whether they would have been equal to their task of repelling the invader. But at least they had been ready to try their best!

GEORGE'S FINEST HOUR

When war broke out in 1939, George Martin debated whether to enlist. He was a fitter at the pit and he knew that he would not have the option for long. The government had learned, during the First World War that it could not afford to allow the manpower of the mines to drain away and would soon stop the recruitment of miners. The idea of life in the forces appealed to George. He was thirty years of age, fit and handsome. He was married to a nice girl and had two lovely children, but there were times when George found life at home a bit tedious. He had a gregarious nature and had always wanted to travel. His wife, on the other hand, was completely domesticated, took wonderful care of the children and made almost a fetish of housework. But, George told himself, she tended to take him for granted and had neglected her appearance a bit since their marriage.

George was still debating what to do when the news came through that one of his friends from schooldays had been killed during the evacuation of the British Expeditionary Force from Dunkirk. That decided George; he would rather have a dull life in the mines than lose it to what appeared a greatly superior enemy.

But in anticipating a boring life ahead, George had failed to recognise the social changes that were taking place around him. The war, and particularly the threat of invasion that now hung over Britain, had begun to generate a new spirit, even among the taciturn inhabitants of South Yorkshire mining villages. People were beginning to loosen-up; they spoke to each other in queues for buses or cinemas; there was more neighbourliness about and, what appealed most to George, there were lots more unaccompanied young women around: there were the wives and sweethearts of young men who had been called up, women doing men's jobs, women who had been conscripted into war work and lots of uniformed ATS girls, WAAFs and WRNS on leave or posted nearby.

Adjacent to the terminus for the buses from town, was a fence enclosing a piece of waste ground, on which George found it congenial to sit for half an hour or so on fine days, usually at the end of the morning shift or before the afternoon shift. He was amazed at the numbers of young women streaming onto and off the buses and it delighted him that some of them began to acknowledge him, cautiously at first, and then to stop occasionally for a chat. They all looked so attractive to George and before long, he was making assignments with the friendlier ones, some of them leading to casual affairs. He was not short of alibis for his absences from home: he was at the allotment; he was at the club; he was fire-watching; he was at a football match and so it went on.

On one memorable day in 1943, George reached his peak. He took the morning shift off work, which he was entitled to do, having earlier worked a double shift to deal with a haulage breakdown. By seven o'clock, he was in bed with Sally, a divorcée, older than himself, whom he had met in a pub. He went home for lunch, complaining about his tiring shift, and then walked the half-mile to his allotment. As he approached, he could see that the curtains of his garden hut were closed and he knew that Ann, a munitions worker from the North, whom he had chatted up at the bus terminus, was waiting for him inside. He would have to get a move on because Ann had to be at the tank factory for the start of the evening shift at four o'clock. After tea, on the pretext of going to the club, he took the bus into town to meet Judy. Judy was a buxom girl from the Midlands, who had been conscripted into the Women's Land Army and posted to a farm on the south side of the town. George had also met Judy at the bus terminus and had soon come to realise that hard physical work in the fresh air had sharpened her appetites and that she was a very exciting woman to be with. After a few drinks in a hotel bar, Judy started to get amorous, whilst George, after his strenuous day, was not sure that he was equal to the situation. But soon, Judy's excitement took hold of him and they made love in the blackout, standing up in a shop doorway.

When George got home around eleven o'clock, he was relieved to find the house silent. The last thing he wanted was Marjorie waking up feeling affectionate; but she had had a tiring day and was sound asleep. Worn out and satiated, George sank thankfully into the bedclothes. His last waking thought was to wonder how long he could sustain his valiant contribution to the war effort.

Bevin Boy

In July 1943, the fuel situation in Britain was so serious that Minister of Labour and National Service, Ernest Bevin, using his powers under the wartime emergency regulations, decided that the manpower requirements of the coal mines should be met by making mining an alternative to serving in the armed forces. However, there were insufficient conscripts volunteering for this option and by December 1943, direction had to be resorted to. One in ten of all conscripts was selected, by impartial ballot, for service in the pits; these reluctant miners came to be known as 'Bevin Boys'.

The ballot was deeply unpopular; university graduates and the sons of professional parents, who had expected commissions in the armed forces, were forced into dirty and dangerous work, in depressing areas of the country, for miserable wages. They had four weeks of desultory instruction, in makeshift training establishments, before being sent underground. The miners regarded the Bevin Boys at best with tolerant amusement and at worst with bitterness. The government expected them to train young men, who did not want to be there, after years of turning a blind eye to the misery of unemployed colliers and their families. The conscripts were herded into quickly thrown-up, nissen hut camps with inadequate heating, unreliable plumbing and served by badly-run canteens. Little wonder that they drank, gambled and sought congenial company wherever they could find it.

Rex Johnson was the only child of loving middle class parents. He lived with his family in Sussex and was taking a well-earned break after graduating from London University. He had qualified for deferment of call-up until he had taken his degree in economics and he had served in the University Air Squadron in the expectation that he would be called into the RAF for flying duties. He could not believe his misfortune when he opened the buff envelope and found that instead, he had been directed to work underground, in a South Yorkshire coal mine, failing which he would go to prison for three months, after which he would be fined five pounds for every day that he delayed reporting for work.

Like the residents of many other mining areas, the villagers had witnessed, early in 1944, the hasty erection of long rows of nissen huts on a disused playing field adjacent to the colliery. On a cold, wet March afternoon, they now watched with mixed feelings as coach after coach disgorged its load of unhappy passengers who, receiving their hut numbers from the officious camp manager, made their way towards their unwelcoming homes. There were twelve beds to each hut. Rex was the first to arrive at the one to which he had been allocated and, noting that the only heating was a single cast-iron coal stove in the middle of the building, chose a bed that was near enough to it to receive some warmth during the cold nights. It was fortunate that he did, because it turned out that in wet weather, the rain tended to blow in around the badly-fitting doors and it was not unusual for those in the end beds to awaken to find themselves surrounded by water.

His intellect sharpened by university tutoring, Rex stood out during the training as the brightest of the intake. In fact, by asking searching questions, he had gained some insight into mining technology and the management of the pit. But despite his obvious intelligence and the interest he had shown, he was disappointed to learn, at the conclusion of his training, that his job for the foreseeable future was to clip full coal tubs onto a haulage rope and to detach empty ones from it. Only the most muscular of his companions made it onto the coal face with its high earnings and Rex remained a haulage hand at three pounds a week. He grew to hate the long trudge to and from his workplace over uneven roads, the choking dust thrown up by tramping feet, the constant stooping to avoid the low roof and the eyestrain of constantly peering through the dim light to see where he was going.

The only congenial feature of life as a Bevin Boy was that Rex and his companions were looked on by the young women of the village as different and interesting young men in a community which had been stripped by conscription of almost all its eligible non-miners. The camp residents were given permission to use the canteen for recreational purposes outside of mealtimes and a social committee was formed to arrange events. Within a very short time, there was some organised activity almost every evening of the week and on Wednesdays and Saturdays the tables were pushed aside, the wooden floor sprinkled with chalk powder and a dance held. There was sufficient musical talent among the inmates to form a small band for these occasions. The villagers were invited, free of charge, and whilst the local men remained aloof, the young women flocked in. The dances were so successful that stories began to circulate in the village about immoral behaviour, but they were false and probably started by the disgruntled male population. The social committee members realised that their very acceptance into village life depended on their good behaviour and any disorderly conduct was quickly dealt with.

University social functions had motivated Rex to learn to dance and he enjoyed the Wednesday and Saturday evenings when his shifts left him free. He became friendly with a hut mate, Ron, from Manchester, and they would sit with a cup of coffee and a cigarette, at a table on the edge of the dance floor, eyeing the young women and comparing notes. They were not as brash or pushy as some of their colleagues and tended not to compete for dances with the more popular girls. Instead, they found themselves attracted to two who were always quietly dressed, not excessively made-up and usually sat well away from where the more predatory males gathered. Rex and Ron got into the habit of having two or three dances with these girls each time they were there and, in the course of a few weeks, became quite friendly with them. Ron's relationship with Angela was never more than a warm friendship, but it soon became clear to both of them that there was a strong attraction between Rex and Sheila. Before long, this attachment reached the stage where the two were meeting, not only at the dance, but elsewhere, on most evenings when Rex was free.

One evening, while Rex and Sheila were dancing, Angela took Ron aside. 'Will you tell me a bit about Rex?' she asked, much to Ron's surprise.

'Why do you want to know about him?' countered Ron, 'What's wrong with me?'

'There is nothing wrong with you, Ron,' replied Angela, 'I like you very much; its just that I care a lot about Sheila and I do not want to see her get hurt.'

'Fair enough,' said Ron and he then told Angela all he knew about Rex and his background, which was all to Rex's credit. 'But why are you so concerned?' he then asked.

'Sheila is ruled by very powerful emotions,' she said, 'I have seen them carry her away before and it is happening again. This past few weeks, she has been like a smouldering volcano.'

Angela then told Ron what lay behind her concern. Shortly after the conscription of women was announced in December 1941, Sheila, who was then twenty-one and working in a shop, was required to register along with all other unmarried women in her age group. At her interview, she was given a choice between the ATS, the WAAF or doing war work in an armaments factory. She chose the WAAF and, after her basic training, was posted to a bomber station in Lincolnshire as an admin assistant. She soon caught the attention of a young sergeant pilot and fell deeply in love with him. She knew all about bomber losses and that he was facing death several nights each month. The combination of her love for him and her fears for his safety robbed Sheila of all restraint and she became pregnant. She hesitated to tell the airman, because of the stress that he was under, and, while she was hesitating, he was posted to another station and he left without saying 'goodbye'. Sheila was discharged from the WAAF on 'family grounds' and returned to the village and a job in the Co-op store. She had a baby boy, who was now almost a year old and was looked after by Sheila's widowed mother.

'So you see,' said Angela, 'I cannot imagine what would happen if Sheila attached herself as strongly to someone else and was let down again.'

'And what would you like me to do about it?' asked Ron.

'Make sure that Rex knows what a vulnerable person she is and warn him that, unless he is sure about his commitment to her, he should back-off rather than ending up hurting her.'

'What about the baby?' asked Ron.

'Tell him about it, but swear him to secrecy,' replied Angela, 'She has to tell him about that herself.'

The following evening saw Rex and Ron sitting in the lounge of the local pub having a heart-to-heart. Rex was deeply touched by what he had heard. He was not yet ready to make a long-term commitment to Sheila, but he knew that he wanted to get to know her better and if possible, to see the baby; but that had to come from her. With gentleness and understanding he gradually encouraged her to open up and, bit by bit, the whole tearful story came out. He could tell that she was relieved at his knowing and was grateful that he did not appear to be turning his back on her.

The spring of 1945 was now approaching and Rex was due to some time off from the pit. Sheila also had some holidays due and she suggested, very tentatively, that they should go away for a few days to somewhere nice where she could forget the past two years and they could enjoy each other's company in peace and quiet. The war in Europe was coming to its end, seaside towns were beginning to clear their beaches of anti-invasion obstacles and hotels were beginning to welcome holiday visitors. They decided on a small hotel above the south cliff at Scarborough and Sheila shyly indicated that she did not expect a separate room.

They arrived by train early in the afternoon and, after booking in, had a walk along the promenade and harbour wall. They returned to the hotel for dinner and then went up to their room. Sheila showered first and when Rex emerged from his, she was sitting up in bed in a pretty nightgown. Rex got into bed beside her in a tumult of conflicting feelings. He wanted her, of course he did; she was beautiful, warm and sensitive. But would it work out? Could he make the necessary commitment? What would his parents say? What about his career that had not yet really started? Was he really what Sheila needed? Could he take on the responsibility of another man's child? Sheila embraced him warmly and made it clear that there would be no holding back. But Rex's conflicting emotions had robbed him of his ardour. He tried to make love, but he couldn't. Sheila's passion slowly turned to distress and she started to weep. Rex tried to explain, but the right words would not come. Finally, he kissed her gently and they turned away from each other. Rex lay awake for most of the night, trying to analyse his feelings and to decide where his future lay. In the early morning, with Sheila still sobbing spasmodically beside him, he had to accept the conclusion that however desirable Sheila was to him and however much he wanted to be with her, it was not enough to overcome his doubts and fears. The following day they cancelled the remainder of their hotel booking and caught the first train home. In the train Rex tried to read, but found himself just staring at the page. A tear trickled at intervals down Sheila's cheek.

Rex put in for a transfer to a pit in the Midlands. For once the wheels of officialdom turned quickly and authority for his move came in less than a month. He waited outside the Co-op at closing time to say 'goodbye' but Sheila must have seen him and gone out through the service entrance at the back.

Rex was fully occupied for a few weeks settling-in to his new job and surroundings. But as soon as he was free to think about other things, he began to realise that he had made a dreadful mistake. He knew now, that he could have been perfectly happy enveloped in the warm love that Sheila had offered him. He knew that, with her at his side, he would have been much better motivated to carve out a career than he now was. He knew that he could have taken to her son and been a good father to him. He also knew that it would now never happen. After a few weeks, he plucked up the courage to write to her, but there was no reply. He later heard from Ron that Sheila had left the village, but no-one seemed to know where she had gone. He finally had to face the fact that he had lost the most wonderful woman that he was ever likely to meet, through his own timidity and indecisiveness, and that memories of her would haunt him for the rest of his life.

Three's a Crowd

Alice Green met Corporal Stan Machin in 1918, on his last leave from France before the Armistice. When Stan was demobilised, he went back to the pit and was soon earning good money as a ripper. They married in 1919 and a year later, Alice had her first baby, a girl. That was the last time that Alice could remember being really happy. She found out that in the last weeks of her pregnancy, when she was too uncomfortable to respond to Stan's advances, he had found solace elsewhere. That was it as far as Alice was concerned. If he had such little respect for her when she was bearing his child, she wanted no more to do with him. But what could she do? Where could she go? Where would the money come from? Times were hard for a woman on her own.

Alice had to compromise. She had lost all feeling and regard for Stan, but he was still her husband and as long as he supported his family and did not mistreat them, she would do her duty as a wife. Doing her wifely duty resulted in three more children, all girls, all within six years. After that, Alice had had enough; she bought a second-hand bed and moved into the bedroom of her two younger daughters.

Alice continued to cook Stan his dinner and pack his snap, but that was all. They hardly ever spoke, unless it was something urgent, and only then in monosyllables. Stan just used the house for eating and sleeping; otherwise, the only time he stayed at home was when he was broke. The girls grew up loving their mother, but completely indifferent to their father. The two older girls married shortly after the outbreak of the Second World War, but because of the uncertainties of the times, neither of them was in a hurry to start a family. By late 1942, all four sisters found themselves working in an armaments factory that had been hurriedly thrown up between the village and the town.

One afternoon, Stan returned home with a much younger woman. He told Alice her name and said she would be staying. It turned out that she had come down from Lanark, looking for her errant husband. She had not found him, but she had found Stan in the pub that he frequented and was apparently ready to do whatever she had to do to secure a roof over her head. Stan thought that his luck was in; he put her suitcase on the bottom stair and threw her ration book on the table. Stan had downed a few and was in an aggressive mood, so Alice thought that she had better bide her time. She gave the two of them a cup of tea and went about her housework. Now Alice's married daughters always called to see her on their way from work to their respective homes, so all four girls arrived together. They kissed their mum, nodded to their father and sat down with a cup of tea to weigh up the situation. Then, with nothing more than a quick glance between them, all four rose together, took hold of the young Scotswoman, bundled her out into the street and threw her suitcase and ration book after her. They then turned on their father. They were big girls and he didn't stand a chance. They punched him, bit him, pulled his hair and kicked him where they knew it would hurt most. They ended with a warning that he would get the same again if he ever tried to do anything of the sort in the future or if he ever laid a finger on their mother.

In the months that followed, Stan became more taciturn than ever He spent even less time at home and often returned the worse for drink. But he never again attempted to pull a stunt like the one he had tried with the young Scotswoman.

Brothers in Arms

The first American soldiers to be seen in the area arrived in the spring of 1943; they were white. They pitched tents and immediately started to build a more permanent hutted camp a few miles from the town. Until the camp was completed they were confined within its perimeter, but as soon as it was up and running they enjoyed the benefit of very liberal leaves and passes and were soon a common sight in the town. With unerring instinct, they sought out the hotels, pubs, cinemas, dance halls and anywhere else that they thought might offer the chance of female company. Groups of them were even to be seen hanging around school gates at home-time. But there was one venue that they missed.

The Astoria ballroom was a former clothing factory, hidden away at the end of a cul-de-sac, which terminated at the canal towpath. The area was run-down and dilapidated and the Astoria itself was a patched-up, single storey building, which showed signs of repeated alterations for the various purposes which it had served in the past. The only thing about it which looked bright and modern was its huge elevated sign which read 'ASTORIA' from top to bottom, in large red letters which, before the blackout, had been illuminated by electricity. But for all its chequered history, the Astoria was bright and cheerful inside. The wooden floor had been sanded and polished for dancing and its perimeter was lined with upright gilded chairs with red velvet seats. There was a refreshment bar in one corner (no alcohol) and diagonally opposite was the master of ceremonies' platform and record player, for there was no live music. What brought young people to the Astoria was its stock of up-to-date records and its completely relaxed atmosphere. A muscular doorman ensured good behaviour, but otherwise there were few rules. In particular, if a couple wanted to try some unorthodox dance steps, there was nothing to stop them, in fact, they were positively encouraged.

In the late summer of 1943, a contingent of coloured Americans arrived at the camp. There was strict segregation between the two races and the newcomers were allocated their own separate accommodation. For the same reason, they had to find entertainment outside the camp that was not already taken over by the white soldiers. They were obliged to look harder and into more obscure areas than their countrymen and, eventually, they discovered the Astoria. The coloured soldiers were not only made welcome at the Astoria, but their style of dancing, especially the 'jitterbug', was a revelation to the locals and was soon being enthusiastically emulated. The girls, in particular, welcomed the black troops; they were so different from any men they had ever met and most of the girls seemed to enjoy being thrown around in the course of the uninhibited dancing. In their enthusiasm for the novel black culture, the girls may have offended the local young men, mainly miners, who may have had some hand in what was shortly to happen.

One September evening a large group of white Americans turned up at the door of the Astoria. The doorman, sensing trouble, told them that the dance hall was full, but they threw money onto his table and pushed their way in. Groups of three or four of them systematically surrounded single black soldiers and proceeded to beat them unmercifully. The girls screamed and the doorman telephoned the police as the fight rapidly escalated. The coloured troops were gradually forced out of the dance hall towards the towpath and the girls with them. Presumably it was the intention to drive them into the canal, but what the whites had not reckoned on was that the towpath was littered with large stones which the girls began gathering and handing to the coloured men. Under a fusillade of stones, the advance of the white troops faltered and then a shrill whistle made them turn around to see a platoon of military policemen with batons drawn. As the MPs rounded up the offending whites, the girls spirited away the black soldiers along the towpath and into a maze of back-streets where they disappeared into the darkness.

A few evenings later, the damage repaired with the aid of a grant from the American commanding officer, the dance hall resumed its peaceful course. But the battle of the Astoria had shown the insular Yorkshire townsfolk a side of American life that few of them had ever suspected and from then on, whenever the hall was open, there were always two armed MPs standing outside the door, as a chilling reminder.

Goodbye to Arms

Tommy Oliver was one of the thousands of young miners who were called for military service at the start of the war, before the government realised that conscription was stripping the pits of irreplaceable colliers and granted them reserved occupation status. Tommy's battalion joined the British Expeditionary Force to help seal the gap at the northern end of the Maginot Line and he and his companions shivered under canvas through the bitter winter of 1939/40 in what came to be known as the 'phoney war'. In May 1940, when the German offensive was launched and Belgium capitulated without warning, Tommy's unit found itself fighting a desperate rearguard action from the Belgian border to the beaches of Dunkirk. It was then exposed to three days of continuous air attack before Tommy and his surviving mates, wading chest-deep in water, were plucked out of the sea by the Royal Navy and deposited, more dead than alive, on the Dover quayside.

Tommy was given a plate of sandwiches, a packet of cigarettes, a fourteen-day leave pass and a rail ticket home. His family were shocked by his gaunt appearance, his sunken eyes and his apparent lack of interest in anything that was going on around him. Try as they might, they could not get him to talk. All the same, they were delighted to get him home in one piece and hoped that a little peace and quiet and some regular meals would soon restore him to the boy that they knew.

But Tommy did not respond to the loving care of his family as they had hoped. True, he began to look better and after a catching up on his sleep, he began to take short walks. He never said where he had been or whether he had spoken to anyone, but the walks became longer and longer and it appeared, from sightings of him by friends and neighbours, that he was roaming the countryside for miles around.

The last day of his leave arrived to find his kitbag, rifle and pack stacked neatly in his bedroom, but no Tommy. When he had not appeared in time to catch his train, his parents, worried out of their minds, informed the police. A search of the village and the surrounding area was made during the course of the following few days, but it revealed no sign of Tommy. Inevitably, the military police became involved for Tommy was now absent without leave and potentially a deserter, but he was still nowhere to be found.

After a few weeks, some of the more adventurous village boys, who tended to roam further afield than the others, began to catch glimpses of a tramp who was new to the area. He had long black hair, a black beard that covered most of his face and wore a scruffy brown overcoat and wellington boots. Whenever the boys came within sight of him he appeared to melt away into the landscape and they never got close enough to speak to him, but they saw enough to notice that his hair and beard were getting longer and more matted and that his clothes were becoming more tattered. Village boys did not discuss with adults what they did or what they saw on their rambles and, in any case, tramps were a common sight in the lanes and byways, so no-one of authority was made aware of the shadowy figure who had joined the itinerant population.

It was a hot August day and a group of boys went down to the river for a swim. Their favourite spot was a safe, waist-deep pool, formed by an eddy under the far bank, where the current turned back on itself. To get there the boys had to wade across a swift, shallow current which flowed into a much deeper pool downstream. But the previous day had been one of summer thunderstorms and heavy rain which had turned the shallows into a torrent. The bigger boys led the way to show that it could be crossed, but when slightly-built Charlie Harris attempted it, he was swept off his feet and carried by the current into the deep pool below. Charlie was a poor swimmer; as the other boys raced along the bank towards him, he thrashed about, trying to stay afloat, but he was fighting a losing battle. Before the boys could reach him, a scruffy figure with a huge beard and long hair emerged from the bank-side bushes, tore off his coat and shirt and dived headlong into the deep pool. He dragged Charlie to the bank, threw him onto his face and began pumping his chest. By the time Charlie had begun to breathe of his own accord, a knot of people had gathered around including two policemen. Realising what would happen next, Tommy Oliver, for that is who the rescuer was, dived once more into the river and stood with water up to his chest, his hair and beard trailing in the current, looking more like some prehistoric cave-man than a member of His Majesty's forces. But there was no escape; more spectators and more policemen arrived and Tommy was eventually coaxed out of the water.

When Tommy's identity had been established, the military police were called and he was taken away on suspicion of desertion. The investigating officers soon realised that Tommy was not well. His replies to their questions were confused and irrational; he was sent to an army hospital where tests soon revealed what was wrong. The retreat from Belgium under constant fire and the days of bombing and strafing on the beach at Dunkirk had caused the sort of neurosis which, in the First World War had become known as 'shell shock'. Instead of being locked up, Tommy received the careful psychotherapy that experience had shown was needed in such cases, after which he was given a medical discharge from the army. He eventually went back to the pit and merged into the community. But a whole generation of village boys remembered Tommy as the tramp who had saved the life of Charlie Harris.

El Cid

Sid White was a boaster and a liar. Everyone who met him soon came to realise what sort of a person he was. Even his mother had to admit it. She used to say to him 'Son, you are a bigger liar than Tom Pepper'. Who Tom Pepper was and how he had acquired such a reputation, no-one seemed to know. In other respects, Sid was quite a likeable chap; he was good company, humorous, generous and would help any of his friends in need, if it was in his power to do so. Now it so happened that one of Sid's friends came to hear about the legendary medieval Spanish hero who, having been mortally wounded, perpetrated the ultimate deception of riding posthumously, at the head of his army, into battle against the Moors, tied to the saddle of his horse. The friend saw something of this bold, illusory character in Sid and began to refer to him jokingly as El Cid; the nick-name stuck.

Sid was born in 1898. He had a sister a couple of years older, but since his mother was forty when she gave birth to Sid, she and her husband realised that he would probably be their only son and they spoiled him. When his romancing became apparent, they scolded him, but they did not have the heart to knock it out of him. Sid left school at fourteen and would have followed his father into the local pit, but his dad did not wish to be embarrassed by his son's dissimulations at work, so Sid went to a colliery in a neighbouring village. He progressed from trapper to screen hand to pony driver, but he did not take to pit life and his lies and exaggerations got him into trouble with the down-to-earth older miners. Sid was sixteen when the First World War broke out and he immediately began trying to enlist, claiming to be eighteen. But he did not look eighteen; if anything, he looked younger than his true age, so he had to bide his time. The day that Sid reached eighteen he went straight round to the recruiting office; what he told the recruiting officers and in what accent, only they knew, but to the surprise of his family and friends, Sid was enlisted into a famous Highland infantry regiment. Within a few weeks he was a Scottish soldier, complete with kilt, sporran and dirk and he had adopted a Scottish accent to suit.

Sid was delighted with his new persona. Not even his baptism of fire in the trenches of eastern France diminished his enthusiasm for the army life and, to give him his due, he turned out to be a good soldier. The only problem was that life in the trenches gave him more opportunity than he had ever had to tell tall stories. His fellow soldiers were a captive audience, who were obliged to sit and listen while Sid embroidered the details of his former life. Equally, during his few home leaves, Sid's friends and drinking companions found it difficult to avoid vivid accounts of his exploits in France.

The eleventh of November 1918 found Sid uninjured and hopeful of staying on in the peacetime army, but the inevitable run-down of the armed services forced his reluctant return to civilian life. With over two million men in the same situation in Britain, the 'land fit for heroes', promised by the government, failed to materialise and there was massive unemployment. After almost a year on the dole, Sid was taken on again at his old colliery. In the meantime he had met Ada, who had been completely captivated by this wonderfully interesting war veteran. With Sid's income reasonably assured, they married, set up home in a council house and began to raise a family. Sid's contribution to the furnishing of the house was a huge enlargement of his photograph, in full Highland dress uniform, which he hung over the living room fireplace, where no visitor could fail to notice it and be impressed.

Most old soldiers are reluctant to talk about their experiences of battle, but Sid suffered from no such inhibitions. His friends and workmates were frequently regaled with highly coloured accounts of trench warfare and Sid's part in it, but he was able to boast with complete truthfulness that he had 'come through it without a scratch'. Sid was proud of that but, in due course, he was given the opportunity to tell a much more heroic tale. On a day excursion to Skegness, the wind began to sweep savagely across the Lincolnshire shore, as it often does, and Sid got sand in his eyes. He did not seek treatment and, after weeks of neglect, his left eye was in a severely infected state. The hospital's eye specialist concluded that the eye could not be saved, so it was removed and a glass eye substituted. From that day on, any new acquaintance was treated to a heart-rending story of how Sid, in the course of a bayonet charge toward the enemy trenches, had been struck in the eye by shrapnel from a shell. In circles where he was not well-known, Sid was a war hero all over again.

Being the man of action and dedication that he obviously was, Sid was often selected to represent his less able colleagues when a spokesperson was needed. He was elected to the branch committee of the mineworker's union, playing a militant role in the General Strike and the protracted miner's strike which followed. He was also voted onto the committee of his local working men's club and became its treasurer. During his treasurership, Sid was never seen without a fat roll of banknotes, bulging from his hip pocket, which he delighted in producing with a flourish, whenever he had to pay out for anything.

When the Second World War broke out in 1939, Sid saw it as an opportunity to get back into the army. He was forty-one but, apart from the loss of one eye, was remarkably fit. Anticipating that, as a miner, he would be in a reserved occupation, he left the pit and took a job as a milkman. He joined the Home Guard on the day that it was formed, in May 1940, and turned up to the first parade in the dress uniform of his highland regiment. To the founding officers, Sid was clearly NCO material and he was quickly promoted to sergeant. He acquitted himself well in the Home Guard, but it was not the army and, as he had done in 1914, he began to importune the recruiting office again. He was told that at his age and with only one eye, he could not be considered. But he continued to pester the recruiting staff and, by mid-1942, with the war going badly for Britain, men in their forties, even with minor disabilities, became acceptable recruits for some non-combatant duties. Sid was offered the Supply Corps and took it gladly. He did his basic training in the Midlands and was posted to a supply depot in Oxfordshire as a Private (Second Class) Stores Assistant.

Glad as he was to get back into the regular army, Sid missed the authority and respect that he had had in the home Guard. It was not long before he had acquired a set of sergeant's stripes and whenever he had leave or a weekend pass, he would sit in the toilet compartment of the train home and quickly sew three stripes on each sleeve of his tunic. He felt much better when he had done that and enjoyed his leave so much more. His family and friends were a little surprised at his rapid promotion, but he was an experienced soldier of the Great War was he not? In the pub or club, Sid would sit on a stool, at a table close to the entrance door, where those coming in could not fail to notice the distinguished-looking sergeant, with his three stripes on his sleeves and his row of Great War medal ribbons on his chest. Sid had one or two narrow escapes from detection by patrolling military policemen, but the risk only added spice to the enormous satisfaction that he derived from his deception.

But it was not that sort of deception that brought Sid down. He took up with a divorcée, a few years younger than himself, who lived in a small town near the supply depot. He learned from her that there was a thriving black market in clothing, household goods and soft furnishings, of which the depot held vast stocks. After three years of war, many everyday domestic items were no longer obtainable and even those that the shops still stocked were subject to rationing on a frugal points system, so there was a ready market for almost anything that could be smuggled out of the depot and Sid's lady-friend had all the necessary contacts. It started with small things like a pair of socks, a vest, a towel, but Sid and his friend gradually became more ambitious. Blankets were in the greatest demand; after three years without replacement most families' blankets had more patches than original material and a new blanket was worth a lot of money. Because of their bulk, blankets were difficult to conceal but, with a little ingenuity, Sid had his share. One day an opportunity came his way that he could hardly believe. The quarter-master sergeant instructed Sid to draw fifty blankets from the store, make a parcel of them and leave it in his room in the sergeant's mess. When Sid asked how the parcel was to be marked, the sergeant replied that it didn't need a label. 'I know what he's up to,' Sid told his lady-friend, 'he's going to flog that lot and make a packet. Well, if he can have fifty, I can have fifty and even if he finds out, he won't dare say anything about it.'

So Sid drew a hundred blankets. He placed fifty of them in a large box which he left unmarked in the sergeant's room and hid the remaining fifty in the roof space of his barrack block, from where he began to withdraw them as and when his friend made a sale. But suspicions had been aroused. Even in such a large depot the shrinkage in the stock of blankets was noticeable and an audit was carried out. Sid was brought up before the QMS and was surprised to hear him speaking quite openly about the fifty blankets he had received. It turned out that the sergeant's order was entirely legitimate, the blankets being needed for the members of a training course who were coming to the depot from other units, so Sid was not able to silence the sergeant by attempting to blackmail him. Enquiries revealed that a brisk trade in army blankets had recently sprung up in the town and it was all traced back to a certain young woman and her soldier friend. Sid was court-marshalled and sentenced to six months in the glasshouse at Aldershot. When he came out there was no longer any place for him in the army and he was awarded a dishonourable discharge. On Sid's return to civilian life, his friends could not detect much of the El Cid left in him.

A Life

Harry Roberts was born in a Nottinghamshire mining village in 1882. His father had been a rural blacksmith, who had moved into the mines as a farrier, because the work was more regular. When Harry left school, at the age of twelve, he started work as a trapper at the same pit as his father. and went on to become a pony driver. On a day that he would never forget, Harry, then seventeen, was called urgently to the stables to learn that his father had been kicked in the head by an agitated pony, which he was trying to shoe. He found his father lying unconscious on a stretcher, where the overman and the ostler were trying to bring him round. There was no response, either to their efforts or to Harry's words of sympathy and reassurance and before they could get him to the surface, Harry's father was dead.

By the time he was twenty-five, Harry was working as a filler on the coal face. His job was to place the coal, which the hewer had broken out, into five- hundredweight tubs. There was a strict Company regulation that filling had to be done by hand. The hewer was paid according to the weight of coal in the tubs that Harry filled, on the assumption that it was all top quality coal and not small coal or slack. Hand filling ensured that the good coal was not degraded by shovelling and that no small coal went into the tubs.

On a black day in 1909, a few minutes before the end of his shift, Harry, in order to clear the stall and get out quickly, shovelled the last of the coal into an almost full tub. But he was spotted by the overman and sacked on the spot. Harry had a wife, Clara, and two children, Billy, aged six and Sarah, four, to support. He asked to see the under-manager and pleaded to keep his job, but in vain. He was told, however, that miners were needed in South Yorkshire, at a new colliery in which the owners of his present pit had an interest. If Harry could present himself at the Yorkshire pit on the following Monday morning, he could have not only a job, but a pit cottage as well. As it was Tuesday, Harry had six days in which to uproot his family and their belongings, travel sixty miles, settle into a new house, in an unfamiliar area, and report for work. He went out and bought a second-hand handcart. By careful arranging, he managed to load it with two beds, a table and four chairs, bedclothes and soft furnishings. Their clothes and personal effects went into two battered suitcases. Their prize possessions: a grandfather clock and a harmonium, were to be sent on by rail, by Harry's mother, when she knew their address.

The family set off early on the Friday morning to walk five miles to the railway station. Harry pushed the handcart all the way, while the children took turns to ride on the cart, in the small space which their father had reserved for them, while Clara helped him to push the cart up the hills. They arrived just in time to buy their tickets and push the cart into the goods van of the waiting train. The train journey was a great novelty for the children who had never travelled by rail before. To while away the time, their father taught them a little song which he had learned as a boy and which suited the occasion:

> Paddy from home had never been,
> A railway train he'd never seen,
> He longed to see the great machine
> That runs along the railway.

The train arrived in the early afternoon and the cart was offloaded without incident. There was no passenger train from the town to the village which was to be their home, so the family prepared themselves for a further four-mile trek with the handcart. On arrival in the village, they went directly to the colliery office to enquire about a cottage, only to be told that there were none available. Harry's heart sank. What could a man do when he found himself with his wife and small children in a strange place, with little money, night coming on and nowhere to sleep? He did the only thing he could do and started knocking on doors to seek temporary lodgings. Almost everyone who answered their knock said that their house was already full or over-crowded, but one or two suggested neighbours who might have room. The cottages had only two bedrooms and, as the pit was new, they were occupied mainly by young families with children who, like the Roberts', had migrated from other mining areas. Eventually, as the light faded and their hearts sank even further, their knock was answered by a young, newly-married couple, Frank and Emily Wilkinson, who had not yet started a family and consequently had a spare bedroom. The room was not large and it was a tight squeeze for the family, but it was a roof over their heads and a temporary relief to their distress.

Harry reported for work the following Monday morning and was relieved to learn that, at least, the promise of work held good. The South Yorkshire coal seams were much thicker than those he was used to in Nottinghamshire and consequently earnings were higher. Clara got the children admitted to the council school, found her way around the village and set about making their temporary home as comfortable as possible. The Wilkinson's were a friendly couple, who did all they could to make the Roberts' welcome and to minimise the inevitable problems of sharing a living room, kitchen and lavatory. Harry was dismayed to learn that the colliery company was not planning to build more cottages in the foreseeable future, but he discovered that a private developer was building terraced houses to rent in the older part of the village where, it was rumoured, a branch railway line was to be laid and a passenger station opened. The rent was within Harry's new earning capacity and, would you believe? the houses were to have gas lighting and bathrooms.

On the day that the Roberts' moved into their new house, there were tearful goodbyes to the Wilkinson's to whom they owed so much, but as their respective houses were less than a mile apart, there were to be frequent visits over the coming years, and as both families grew, both parents and children became lifelong friends.

Harry worked on the coal face at the same pit for twenty-five years. During that time, he was badly injured twice by falls of stone. On both occasions, when he was discharged from hospital, he was sent to a miner's convalescent home to regain his health and strength: once to a home on the North Yorkshire coast and once to another in rural Bedfordshire. With the exception of day trips to the seaside, these were the only times in his working life that Harry left home. Borrowing a bicycle, he made the most of his opportunity to explore the countryside in both locations. Being a gregarious sort of chap, he made firm friends of several fellow-inmates, with whom he subsequently kept in touch for many years. He never tired of telling his family and friends about his experiences at the convalescent homes.

By the early 1930s, many years of inhaling coal dust and stone dust were beginning to tell on Harry. He was beginning to have difficulty with his breathing and he never felt really well anymore. In 1934, on his doctor's advice he decided to leave the pit. His son, Bill, was out of work, so they decided that they would rent a plot of land and, between them, run a market garden; Bill would do the heavy work, whilst Harry would look after the greenhouses and do the marketing and office work. Building up the trade was slow but, with hard work, they eventually began to show a profit, and by the time the war started, in 1939, they had a successful business.

In 1940, Bill was called up into the army, but Harry found an older chap to replace him in the garden and carried on with what he regarded as a valuable contribution to the war effort. But, in 1941, under the wartime emergency labour regulations, Harry was directed back into the pit. He was then fifty-nine and in poor health. He appealed against the direction and went before a medical tribunal who, in their wisdom, decided that Harry was not fit for work underground, but was capable of surface work. Harry was put to work on the coal grading screens, where the atmosphere was dustier than anywhere underground and which, for anyone with respiratory problems, was the worst possible working environment. Harry stuck it out as best he could, despite several bouts of severe illness, but by the autumn of 1944, he no longer had the breath to walk to the pit and he was released.

Harry was not to have the joy of seeing the end of the war nor the return home of his son. He died in the February of 1945 at the age of sixty-three. His death certificate recorded the cause as 'respiratory failure'; it made no mention of the fatal combination of mine dust and blind officialdom that had really killed him.

CPSIA information can be obtained
at www.ICGtesting.com
Printed in the USA
LVOW12s1307150317
527314LV00001B/83/P